I0633180

MINIATURES

Günther Kaip

Translated into English by

Hillary Keel Strohmeier

Matthias Goldmann

Interactive Press
an imprint of IP (Interactive Publications Pty Ltd)
Treetop Studio • 9 Kuhler Court
Carindale, Queensland, Australia 4152
sales@ipoz.biz
http://ipoz.biz/shop
First published by IP in 2024
© 2024 Günther Kaip (text); IP (design)

All rights reserved. Without limiting the rights under copyright reserved
above, no part of this publication may be reproduced, stored in or introduced
into a retrieval system, or transmitted, in any form or by any means
(electronic, mechanical, photocopying, recording or otherwise), without the
prior written permission of the copyright owner and the publisher of this
book.

Printed in 14 pt Avenir Book on Caslon Pro 12 pt.

ISBN: 9781922830708 (PB) 9781922830715 (eBook)

A catalogue record for this
book is available from the
National Library of Australia

Introduction

These prose pieces originally appeared in German in *Im Fluss* Klever-Verlag 2008 (In the Flow), *Im Fahrtwind* Klever-Verlag 2010 (In the Airstream), *Im Rhythmus de Räume* Klever-Verlag 2012 (In the Rhythm of Spaces), and in *Rückwärts Schweigt die Nacht*, Klever-Verlag 2022 (The night is silent backwards).

I am grateful to Ralph Klever and his Klever-Verlag https://klever-verlag.com for allowing me to have "miniatures" from the above books translated into English and published by Interactive Press, Australia.

Some of the pieces appeared in English in *Unbraiding the Short Story*, anthology of the 14th International Conference on the Short Story in English, Vienna, 2014, and online at https://wordcitylit.ca/2021/12/15/miniatures-by-gunther-kaip-translated-by-hillary-keel/

The cover drawing is by Günther Kaip.

The pieces were translated from German into English by Hillary Keel Strohmeier (HKS)and Matthias Goldmann (MG).

Hillary also translated Günther Kaip's take on how he approaches his work (the original German appears together with three of his "miniatures" in the German-language anthology, *Austr(al)ia*) https://www.flodobooks.com/product/australia-prosa-aus-australien-und-osterreich/

"Straight lines from A to B do not exist in our consciousness, which is constantly under attack by its impressions and experiences: seeing, smelling, tasting, hearing, feeling. They sometimes seem to have nothing to do with each other in the text, a juxtaposition of impressions, existing singularly, though they do form a whole. In memory it is words, which

awaken, combine, trigger emotions, and suddenly direct to a new path, leading to different locations of the experienced. It's the famous 1+1=3! Only instead of numbers, the word unifies.

Words have a body, a sounding board, permanently vibrating and creating spaces in this movement, which stretches out, nar s, and multiplies itself further—stories arise in this word rhythm, plots are traced, broken off and newly established. Windows of perception merge seamlessly as well as the internal and external view.

My short prose pieces deal with the variety and simultaneity of spatial experiences in language, which I want to make to a tangible experience, to movement in the text of its language and words, which at best provoke new perceptions and perspectives in its readers."

I hope this book will introduce the work of Günther Kaip to English-language readers.

– Sylvia Petter

Interactive Press

Miniatures

Günther Kaip was born in Linz in 1960 and moved to Vienna in 1980 where he writes full time. His work has been published in anthologies, literary journals and magazines and includes poetry, short stories, novels, children's books, clay structures and drawings. Kaip also works for Austrian National Radio ORF, and Germany's NDR. He has been awarded several prizes and scholarships for his work which has been translated into English, Russian, Polish, Spanish, and Turkish. He is a member of GAV, Austria's largest writers' association.

Originally from Herkimer, New York, **Hillary Keel** (HKS); 1959-2022) was a poet, performer, and translator. Hillary lived in Austria from 1982 to 2009, where she studied at the Schule für Dichtung (sfd/Vienna Poetry School). In 2009, Hillary completed her MFA in Creative Writing at Jack Kerouac School of Disembodied Poetics, Boulder, Colorado. She continued to work as a poet, hypnotist, translator and adjunct for German and the German Fairy Tale at Hunter College in New York City until her death in 2022.

Matthias Goldmann (MG) is a writer and translator based in Vienna, Austria. He has published essays, poetry, and stories, created and exhibited computer text animations, and cooperated with visual artists and authors on various projects and publications. He has worked as an editor with academic publishing companies for several years and has translated numerous publications for publishing houses, museums, artists, and authors in Austria, Germany and the US.

Interactive Press
Brisbane

Photo: Ute Damisch

Contents

Introduction · v

from *In the Flow* · 1

At that time (HKS) · 3
The location (HKS) · 4
The voice (HKS) · 5
Morning mood (HKS) · 5
Now (HKS) · 6
Tomorrow (HKS) · 6
With the hammer (HKS) · 7
Different music (HKS) · 7
Take your shoes (HKS) · 8
Loss (HKS) · 8
A dwelling arises thus (HKS) · 9
Nighttime Blues (HKS) · 9
Clumsy (HKS) · 10
Animal Crossing (HKS) · 10
Restructuring (HKS) · 11
Homecoming (HKS) · 11
The burning moon (HKS) · 12
The cloud compressors (HKS) · 12
Stars (HKS) · 13
Grief (HKS) · 13
The forest and you (HKS) · 14
After the shipment (HKS) · 15
For a blink (HKS) · 15
I devour gardens (HKS) · 16
Dalliance (HKS) · 16
What I meant by that... (HKS) · 17
Evening all afternoon long (HKS) · 17
The cleverest (HKS) · 18
Lavish dish (HKS) · 18
The ogre (HKS) · 19
His body machine (HKS) · 19
The future horror (HKS) · 20
Depression (HKS) · 21
Deceased for the fourth time (HKS) · 21
Positioned (HKS) · 22
In broad daylight (HKS) · 22
Evening (HKS) · 23
Epilogue (HKS) · 24

from *In the Airstream* · 27

The years' picture (HKS) · 29
The night eaten (HKS) · 29
The matter is not straightforward (HKS) · 30
Reconciliation (HKS) · 30
100 grams (HKS) · 31
Authenticity's absence (HKS) · 31
Nothing but meaningless reincarnations (HKS) · 32
The acquaintance (HKS) · 32
The row of trees (HKS) · 33
A night of broken pieces (HKS) · 34
The cube (HKS) · 34
The light pump (HKS) · 35
To calm itself (HKS) · 35
The transitions lack cues (HKS) · 36
The street there (HKS) · 36
We all walked out into life (HKS) · 37
The rigid convictions (HKS) · 37
Whoever this life (HKS) · 38
Before your eyes (HKS) · 39
This certain thing (HKS) · 40
A curved glass cabinet (HKS) · 41
My friends... (MG) · 42
Wire entanglement (MG) · 43
Legs and arms (MG) · 44
Storm of rays (MG) · 45
The background in the foreground (MG) · 46
Fish (MG) · 47
Bodies on the water (MG) · 48
The young twigs (MG) · 49
Electric shocks (MG) · 49
They just sit there (MG) · 50
Beginner and advanced skills (MG) · 50
Water running from your ears (MG) · 51
The proof (MG) · 51
A handful of sand (MG) · 52
Columns of displaced persons (MG) · 53
Saved-up eternity (MG) · 54
One fine day (MG) · 54
A promising start (MG) · 55

Reconciliation with rocks (MG) 56
Drink the flesh (MG) 56
In reality (MG) 57
Climb higher (MG) 57
The first night (MG) 58
You sleepy child (MG) 58

from *In the Rhythm of Spaces* 59

The Morning (MG) 61
Too Late (MG) 62
First Meeting (MG) 63
An environment (MG) 64
These dreams (MG) 65
In the shadow of the dream (MG) 66
The Folding Pattern (MG) 67
Oh, the crackling (MG) 68
Inlays (MG) 69
Found turns of words (MG) 70
You've Cried Enough (MG) 71
When He Wanted to Get Up (MG) 72
At the Head of the Mattress (MG) 73
My Country's Horizon (MG) 74
The Shadows (MG) 75
Death Has Long Been
Intruding (MG) 76
The Breath Slinger (MG) 77
Cross-Stitches (MG) 78
In the Morning (MG) 79
The Empty Space (MG) 80
The Body Fans Out (MG) 81
Part of the Protocol (MG) 82
Just This Handful of Things (MG) 83
The Thought (MG) 84
The Soup (MG) 85
Deathday (MG) 86
I carry my shadow (MG) 87
Literal Bewilderment (MG) 88
First Body Swap (MG) 89
Jackknife dive (MG) 90
We Race Across the Viaducts (MG) 92
The Last Message (MG) 93
Minutes Later (MG) 94
Isn't it Strange? (MG) 95
From hearsay (MG) 96
The Heart (MG) 97
A Dinner (MG) 98

A Clean Sweep (MG) 99
It's High Time (MG) 100
Every Rhythm (MG) 100
He Who Calls Himself God (MG) 101
The Day of Your Birth (MG) 102
Take The Feather from
The Ox (HKS) 103
The Body at the River (HKS) 105

from *The night is silent
backwards* 109

Booby traps and other
ribaldries (HKS) 111
Breach of contract (HKS) 112
Making inhabitable (HKS) 113
Establishing (HKS) 114
Welcome change of pace (HKS) 115
Swift contemplation (HKS) 116
The soul's gravity (HKS) 117
A protocol (HKS) 118
Conversation with Stones (HKS) 120
They really exist (HKS) 121
And this, too (HKS) 122
Passwords (HKS) 123
No property (HKS) 124
Expectation (HKS) 125
Preparing salmon (HKS) 126
In The Machinery Room (HKS) 128
No Mere Hunger (HKS) 129
Capsizing (HKS) 130
Differences (HKS) 131

Publication of Miniatures since... 132

from *In the Flow*

At that time

I remember the dresses' smell of fish, the caravans without counsel, the hot beaches, the taciturn lanterns assembling every night along paths, the remains of temples from the crumbling crescent moon, the white sky, and its dirty rags. I remember how I stood awestruck in this setting, my right hand raised and ready to wave a flag cloth, and I yearned to bury myself in leaves and to bed slaughtered calves on my belly so I could finally fall asleep in their wake.

The location

It's rumbling at the location. Its hiccup chases shadows into the country and light gusts of wind finally carry them off. Soon the first exhausted ones will also be hastily buried. Reasons as far as the eye can see. On a case-by-case basis, the location will hang on a tree in front of the window as soon as tomorrow. Its discourses to the snow, the embarrassment of these soothe me. I join company with it and take a seat on it. It doesn't give me any assignment, leaves further steps up to me, spans the bridges from a to b and has them subsequently ending nowhere. Hands lie naked in the snow. They shovel snow for hours.

One easily becomes suspect as a fanatic searching for the words' miserable hideouts. This is also an advantage to my position. The suspect remains suspicious und is ultimately nowhere to be found. That's why this location where I've resided for two weeks has grown dear to me.

If I graze a wall, then I'll also graze a second, a third, a fourth. Light falls through the cracks. Warm light swirling with particles of dust. Before bedtime, the fields freeze into sleep, face and ears floating on the echoes of night. Life and death mean nothing here. The bright areas have become frequent.

The voice

The weather conditions suffer from a rough icy area. A red skirt brushes over the snow, swirling up the surrounding dreams. The mosses sink in the underbrush and set their traps. Trees punish the birds with their disdain. A springtime memory lisps its shadow pattern into the frozen lake with new tenderness. A rabbit knots its paws and rolls across the glacier, which lies in white reverence. A rift falls there from the sky, scarring every crag.

Morning mood

The paths lead immediately through the forest, tripping in place, for miles. Meadows roll out and get lost in the distance, surveying the sky. Boxes and cartons are ready, the wind wraps itself around every tree and leaves strangulation marks in the bark. Moss piles up everywhere and offers itself for sale. A stream wants to meet his sleep, but seeps away halfway. A flower of style. A multiplication table of the adopted weights. All artfully tied. Ready to ship.

The forest wearily lays its green on the meadows and fields. The sky rumbles down the valley in the boxes and cartons. The trees shake the wind from their trunks and banish it from the land.

Now

Nothing helps. No cowbell on a pasture in bloom. No
before and after. It stays. Everything. The scream comes
from the archive. The undulating wheatfields are the sighs
setting in. The blades of grass bounce in the wind and attract
dragonflies. Deer quarrel with rabbits over testimony in the
forest close by; the only genuine one, etched once into tree
bark, will endure for years. The sun rolls leisurely behind the
hills, the moon shifts its inspection lamp. Several trees step
from the darkness of the forest and draw figures in the wind.
Out of practice, it blows itself up and deflates. The pause
extends—and shoe heels clomp on the blooming pasture as
the sun sets.

Tomorrow

Tomorrow we will regret everything, disclose dreams.
Milestones will blunder in our hearts and break to pieces.
We will clean and oil the rifle barrels again. The hills will
saddle themselves in green, erect trees, entice the winds to
their branches. They will caress each other and lay out their
presumptions, wink at us—encouragingly—but nothing will
help. In our hearts new milestones will form a pile so high
that it leaves the sky speechless. Dreams will applaud and
stare at the gun barrels. Then the triggers will be pulled.

With the hammer

I smash the winds with the hammer. The weather promises
to turn good. A drowned pilgrim is just floating by. That's
half of the opposite. One must keep this in mind. Only with
new rules can one veer onto a new path, otherwise every new
direction would have the same meaning. Should one turn
around, one reads in the air that wind tunnels in the future
will be built narrower.

Different music

How many vows do we need? We hand them out to the
naïve from the hawker's tray, we give them as presents to
the shrewd. The gods don't swoop in to help us, they swarm
ahead to the toilets and argue who goes first. While we
cradle our hips, lay our head at the nape. Choose different
music, Mozart, Shostakovich, Satie – and this opens itself to
a narrow clearing. Directly ahead of us.

Take your shoes

Take your shoes, dear ones. The floor is hot here. The
fire department has closed and gone to bed with the
extinguishing water, begetting fire sources. Watch out for
the fragments of ice hanging in the air. It's best you lubricate
them with your saliva. Walk next to the street in knee-high
grass. It smells of lost recipes and canceled dinner parties. Be
cautious. This is the sweat made of anger and grief, it throws
its image on the horizon, holding position with a groan: its
white is blinding and shifts like a tongue in the landscape.
Only crows may circle above it. In the meantime, the new
day is postponed so you can dedicate yourselves completely
to your shoes. Take them in your hands since they are weary
of your feet. The fire department is in flames. Put your shoes
down and go barefoot.

Loss

And then he already has it. It's to laugh at, he thinks
and disappears at the next house corner. He looks for an
accommodation in the day. He smells the river close by.
His rejoicing is composed of a handful of water. He lost his
ticket. He will get drunk with this handful of water until the
evening lies beside him and it dazes him with its fragrances
and scents.

A dwelling arises thus

Two square cells. That's enough for now. Above that are four tracks of detours woven with interrupted negotiations, garnished with devastated evenings, the sweat of wooden beams on all this. Several snow stars then sprinkled on top, shake everything fiercely—and done!

Nighttime Blues

Three omissions before the answer. It's been lying on the table for years and stinks. Pure whimsey. An invocation knocks gently on the windowpane; an entreaty becomes a prayer. Two omissions roll from the table and shatter on the floorboards. The third shudders from the stench of death, pulls it over the tabletop. The answer follows. They fall onto the floorboards, but don't shatter; they double over as is proper for the answer and the omission. The prayer shifts the room into vibration, the windowpane plinks.

Clumsy

They swerve into the arms of the other. Into the tiniest particulars. Their supple mouths quiver in the frenzy and their throats overflow with curses. Fingers sashay, tickle, prick skin, hands grab between thighs, into armpits, encompass throats, knead breasts and bellies, press heads, expand them—all this in one embrace.

Animal Crossing

Belief grows in the days outside. Three times around the tree trunk and once into the branches. Bury the head in the ground. The lungs till the inhaled air. The formation is in the body's murmuring and its blood vessels. The daily program is thereby determined as an exception. Workhours should be adhered, vigorous turns and immediate pleasures. Acquaintanceships rule the spaces and gaps. A card game is handed out. The soup then spoons itself into the food. Faith mounts itself under the tabletop, a prayer knocks at the table leg. Hardly time to fall asleep. Generators are fired up in the yard. Cliques arranged, and nighttime is driven from the barn.

Restructuring

When the war has ended, the cemetery will be newly
arranged. The bustling gained thus will indulge in pieces
of knitting. Experts in human nature, experts in God will
appear with tooth gaps in their beard. Boiling water will
stand at the ready on every street corner to rinse the souls, to
remove their coughs. Intestines will be handed out, brains,
through which a deep rupture extends. Starving fish will
come on land, saunter through the streets, and cram their
mouths with food. On the side, they will tamper with their
account balances, increase their weight. They will tremble
from the cold, spray blood from the plastic pouches draped
around. A wooden leg will come by and holds the child's
hand. The wooden leg and the child, they will walk to the
cemetery to marvel at the new arrangement.

Homecoming

See the homecoming in the background, bent over, the tip
of its nose is almost on the ground. It's hauling it's battered
suitcase behind it. Stickered with a palm beach. The first frost
is already upon us. Marks in the snow draw the boundary.
Between them the bent over figure. A dormant lake until the
tree line where the crag begins. We, the ones returning home,
sit on a rock and let our legs dangle, place bets whether the
homecoming is just beginning or has already occurred, or
whether it only just wants to look in on us for a quick visit.

The burning moon

The white christening robes wrap themselves around the tree
trunk in the park. Their tails flutter in the wind, brush over
the faces of those walking by. It is evening. The full moon in
the sky burns. It needs quiet. The stars watch indifferently
and get lost in assumptions. The walkers see the stars'
complaint in the sky, walk further, rub their eyelids, and look
at their path, walk further and forget the burning moon, the
stars. The christening robes disentangle from the tree trunks,
flutter in the wind toward the moon, the stars.

The cloud compressors

The cloud compressors are switched off. Any further use
is out of the question tonight. The curses above die out.
Departures flare up, illuminate the night. It becomes bearable
under these circumstances; but then the night gets lost
among unripe apples and chicken coups and shirts drenched
with sweat: it accuses us of being guilty. Of course, we wring
our hands. Scream or fall to the ground. Where we sit and
stand, just now. Rather pathetic, right? But this consistency!

Stars

The stars are buttons in the velvet of night, which billows out into the wind, that speeds over our heads, gets ensnarled in tree branches and breaks. Electricity pylons take part, leaves on the street, meadows, and fields. What remains in place here are our dreams, their finely woven fabric, which wraps itself around night to reach the stars, reminding of radiant hearts.

Grief

The fleas that escaped stand at the back door. In view of the grief, the abyss remains. Perhaps two interlocked hands, a slender neck, and no sleep. This connection has persisted for days. Crinkled sheet metal wrapped around the tree trunk and threads of blood reach into the earth realm. All is disheveled, including the dispersed demonstration. A door is slammed shut by the wind, a roar penetrates the forest, raises up the body and jolts the skull, grabs at the back of the head, and hits it against the tree trunk, over and over again. Two hands disentangle themselves from each other, measure the distance to the heartbeat, which is just unpacking its sewing machine.

The forest and you

And then look. You see the hill with wheatfields in the distance, ahead of that the small forest, where a thin column of smoke rises, twisting higher and higher into the air. You stand in the brook up to your knees, there's no bank. But it is really a brook. I looked it up in the encyclopaedia. Consulted witnesses.

Don't let this get you down. No one can take your vast view of this landscape from you. Your love of it, the fizzy sound in your breast, where your heart pumps blood through your body. Low-hanging branches dip their tips into the water, a wooden board floats by. And you stand in the mud, in this brook, you see the glow of fire in the forest, above it black clouds of smoke. Concentrate now, shut your eyes, listen to the brook, to the wheatfields' waving in the wind, far away but still close. Now open your eyes, see the forest, no more column of fire above it, you dreamt that, like everything you dream, while you don't go into the forest. Go barefoot, so the mud has room between your toes.

After the shipment

Do you know what you have to do after the shipment of
steam-driven feelings, after the gentle fraternizing with
the clouds' electricity, hand in hand with notable years on
shoulders, which you call your own, and after the forbearance
of your heroic death, flowing in small rivulets to the valley
while you pace the upper deck in your latitudinal and
longitudinal lines—do you really know what you'll do
next? Or will you continue to contribute to the mystical
speculations at coffeehouse tables—mornings, evenings,
nights—even your sleep is an abstraction.

For a blink

Two days later he takes a step forward. Everywhere on earth
it's like this. Or one back. That is no mistake, since the pause
is heard everywhere, others say they hear the mistake. On
every street corner. The mistakes always sit there and stare
at the passers-by. Then they even begin to jabber, crowd
into the head, on shoulders, creep into underwear, play shoe
insoles, lure to dark street corners. If he would just take a step
forward, he could silence the jabbering and concentrate on
the visible. Mindfully and slowly look around for a blink.

I devour gardens

I devour gardens with glee. Down to the stumps, and with style. Till plant juice trickles from my mouth combined with my own saliva. Maybe, too, the sun within arm's reach, a glowing wafer; breaking off a piece, I place it on my tongue. That's splendid. Then my hands are free, and I tear roots from the earth, stuff them inside me until I vomit them up, while the glowing nest of sun expands in my belly. Sometimes razor sharp. Sloshing up and down, it gets lost in my legs. This domesticity! This desire! I deploy every conceivable ruse. And I continue—until my gums, eyes, and all my organs lie down in the same bed, and I press the sun tightly onto my breast.

Dalliance

Exert your gaze to your hands. One last time. You have surrounded it with hills and taken all the light. You converse with your own echo. It's been this way for hours. You should finally see your face. It's completely haggard because you don't pay it any attention. Above you in the sky—the stars—none of them stay their course. But they don't fall to Earth. They blink at you, you think, a message just for you. You old dreamer. Take it to the finish; anyway, that will all vanish soon.

What I meant by that...

What I meant is that I put up with it, at the moment. The tarpit stumbles by on its knees and steams like crazy. It's sloppy. It's angry. It stinks. The lawn airs its burning areas and mixes poison in its smoke. The damp sheets on the laundry line flutter in the wind. Even the chimney on the roof or the cumulus clouds in the sky. Everything flutters. Of course, it would be a simple matter, to wrap the thing just depicted in a psychological constraint, to place it in the gaps between words, or to smear it between the individual sounds into a sound paste. These are the circumstances in which breath takes itself away, by this I meant to say that it doesn't keep its promise. Everything flutters.

Evening all afternoon long

It is evening all afternoon long, and three hours prior it was still morning, but the afternoon works itself into the foreground: stuttering its text, threatening with night, displeasing the morning, of course, since it's morning's turn. So, it approaches the evening, cowering in the background, and the midmorning, tending to its wounds, and to noon, stowing away its cutlery—all four put the afternoon in its place, and resolve to leave it alone, to suspend its texture, which only yields breathlessness and disorientation, leading to the afternoon contesting its own position.

The cleverest

The cleverest part about my ignorance are its attacks of
weakness, which run its saddle horse to death; of course, my
ignorance forgets to cover itself, remains naked, simply naked
and gapes. Indifferent to where it stands or goes. It flourishes
easily in meadows, shines among the grasses, and thinks no
one can see it.

Lavish dish

The cooking time amounts to half an hour. This creates a
sense of relief and promotes concentration on the essentials.
Cut everything into slices and let simmer in one litre of
water, enough time to begin the cleaning of finger and
toenails. Afterwards, the cleaning of teeth with a new
toothbrush, but without the application of toothpaste. One's
own saliva is sufficient. For best results, this is completed
while standing and with the eyes shut, while the water in the
pot on the stove begins to seethe, surging against the walls
of the pot, forming bubbles. In case music is on hand, move
the pelvis gently in time, pitter-pattering the feet in position.
Pay no attention to the cooking time, it will evaporate. Then
dive into the atmosphere, don't be surprised when damp heat
rises to your face, but continue to breathe and take a whiff
of what's boiling up. Now, toss the herbs finely chopped
beforehand into the pot, stir with a wooden spoon, and turn
off the stove. Wait till the soup has cooled off, wait, wait, and
… in case you have not fallen asleep, slurp the soup, until you
are happily weary of it.

The ogre

The ogre makes use of the thread mechanism, from which his soul hangs. He cuts his hair and plucks his eyebrows. The mouth remains small, the cheeks hollow. He begins to chew a stone. This sets all animals in flight but lures the humans. They come out from their caves and spread their arms. The ogre turns his head and beckons the first human with a wave of the hand. He runs like a somnambulist across sharp stones, directly into the arms of the ogre. They embrace each other tightly, their vertebrae crack.

His body machine

Now he stands up, now he hears, now he speaks, now he smells, now he feels tired—that should have been for the last time. He can't remember anymore, while his body machine rides to its top floor. En route, he disembarks, buys himself wooden heels and taps through wide halls full of twittering birds. Then he continues the ride up. A sad starry animal comes by and gives him no look of acknowledgment. He disembarks again. A tree trunk lies three steps ahead of him in the sun. Dew drops glitter on blades of grass. Sand dunes in the distance. On the gravel path ahead of him a pile of visored caps. He takes one. Then he tears his mouth open, places the cap on his head and takes one step back, gets into the elevator car again and rides to the top floor. Stepping from the elevator car, he hears the hush.

The future horror

The future horror is wrapped around a rod and carried on display. The lips press a line into the face. The remaining body is buoyant and light. After three steps an elegant cradling of the hips. A red carpet underneath feet.

The rod rushes ahead in a straight posture—there's nothing left to do. The future horror's rags come loose, blow in the wind, wrap around the ears of those waiting, clog them. Past damp houses. They stare with their windows onto the street, watching the rod pursued by a small black, leather suitcase. The hand dangling from the handle once carried it to train stations, into tunnel tubes, across meadows and fields. Once, the suitcase was tied down on a back, carried to the peak of a mountain in a heavy snowfall. The suitcase and its hinges stood frostbitten next to the shabby summit cross. How it returned, it does not know anymore, it doesn't matter, since it is trying to keep up with the rod: both jump across railway tracks to reach the open field. But the suitcase dashes onto the tracks and opens. Snow billows from the insides, freshly fallen snow. However, the rod does not stop, it rushes over the first hill, towards the future horror.

Depression

The depression celebrates triumphs in its tent, gets hammered, puts everything into its mouth, anything it finds, salivates it to mishmash. It can't swallow it, rolls it from one row of teeth to the other, coats its tongue. The depression has been running in circles in the tent with its mouth glued shut, while the forest burns down outside, a murder takes place one hundred meters from the tent and the sky hangs in shreds not taking in any of that. Just now it's biting through the support rod in the tent's roof.

Deceased for the fourth time

At the age of 30, he died for the fourth time, which he took with a sense of calm; even the relatives, the wife, and friends from his childhood days keep calm and wait for the third day after his death, when he should re-emerge, as always, as if nothing happened. Three days pass—nothing happens. The fourth day follows—nothing happens. The relatives and wife and friends become restless. They speak to each other on the telephone in tears, choking for words. The fifth day follows— nothing. They speak on the telephone again. Some no longer in tears. The sixth day comes—nothing. And so it goes, day after day. He remains dead. Even the living relatives, the wife and friends, will die sometime. Everything will take care of itself. The 30-year-old, still considered to be dead, and deceased for the fourth time, notices this with a sense of relief.

Positioned

To escape the experience of failure, sleep ambushes him in
a timely manner, pulling itself over his head. All valves are
shut. It is inherently ordinary. It sabotages perception. He
will lie for a long time among the boxes, the ones he carried
home all afternoon long from the supermarket yesterday.
With a hanging tongue, and armpits wet with sweat. With
trembling legs and burning lungs. As he shoved the last box
with his foot into the workroom, he saw the sky through
the narrow door crack behind the window. It was blue, and
somewhere the sun remained hidden. Then he set himself in
position.

In broad daylight

Stars blossom in broad daylight, the tips of grass shake
dewdrops to the earth, trees from the nearby forest lean
on each other. A bird shakes golden seeds from its wings,
heads of walkers pass by with carefully combed hair, a
hand scratches open the path's asphalt, until the stones are
exposed. A black hat plays pin the tail on the donkey with
blue woollen gloves, the brook close by collects sunrays and
transforms into a bright ribbon, while the shadows flee to
the forest's darkness and call for help. Empty words become
decisive doubters, and the wind seals everything with its
breath, transforms itself into a storm and jolts and joggles
everything, drives it directly out to the horizon.

Evening

Store the evening right behind the rain barrel. Spread it out, brush it, touch it softly: then it should settle down and rest. Perhaps, beforehand, you'll bring it a cup of light, just this one. Does it stare at you? Yes? Before long it will have found its street of porcelain. Give it a kiss on its forehead. So, it remembers, remembers heaven, remembers Earth, remembers us.

Epilogue

If someone asks, what he did today, he will answer thus:

I went to unknown quarters of the city, stretched my arms up to ease tension, and tickled the sky's belly,

… painted new horizons with all colours of the wind, while I waded in the fountainhead of the world circling around me,

… questioned my eyes about their genuine intentions,

… stopped in front of ground floor windows and leaned my fervent forehead onto the window glass,

… set furrows discreetly in my forehead and smoothed them out again with the next thought,

… put the display windows on the shopping promenade in new frames and carried them to the other side of the street,

… rolled an apple with a bite taken out under a newspaper and waited to see whether one of the passers-by would discover it,

… bent down to books in a bookshop and listened to their whispering for hours,

… invented flowers for my hands and followed them, exhilarated, into the sun,

… caressed the flowers and thereby enlivened my shy expression, which naturally undermined this moment,

… recited my thoughts out loud to myself, which toddled blindly behind me,

… wove stardust, because I felt like it,

… spread it out over the part of the city where I found

myself, and rejoiced over the shining eyes of children, followed their expressions playfully immersing into the stardust,

... released the noise from a condemned house and dragged it along behind me,

... loaded myself with the odours of houses and humans that obstructed my way, which I immediately shouldered and was able to shake off at the city egress,

... heard the trees' rustling and all at once, comprehended their secret affinities,

... ran across the lake to the other bank to rent a rowboat,

... crept into the heart of a woman passing by in hiking clothing, listened to the soughing of her blood, and then let myself plop out again onto the dusty path,

... sent a registered letter to two angels, invoking them to more consideration,

... seduced a blind person to see,

... sent fate some shadows from its past,

... did not shy from the narrow scurrying path, which led around the lake, and the wind, which tousled my hair,

... took a step every second, jumped from stone to stone and finally outran myself,

... lay under yellowed leaves in the forest and counted time,

... clicked my tongue and found myself in my bed,

... tore open the drawers to my night table, wherein crumpled mattresses and stretched sheets lay,

... licked the mirror's nakedness on the wall cabinet and made note of its taste on a piece of paper,

… smoked opium as a distraction,

… mourned the flaring fire wiped up yesterday by the cleaning lady,

… slept in my memories and let days and nights pass by,

… went gaga for an hour,

… tripped up every dog running by before I sank back into my dreams,

… looked for shelter in birds' nests,

… sucked dew from blades of grass,

… stood in front of star clusters and complimented them on their magnificent color, which was other-worldly,

… gave the pasture my heart-grass as a present, which the cows dunged with their cow flop,

… drummed on the back of the evening with two fists, until it gave up its chairmanship and made room for the night,

… pulled my ear and admonished myself to be patient and then, then I put myself to bed and fell asleep.

from *In the Airstream*

The years' picture

Today the years picture their life more clearly. Namelessly they kindle embers in the morning, have their discontent from the past days mark their time and walk aimlessly about. The sun's shimmer is ghostly on the world, eyes ache in this diffused light. The outlines of the next things are hard to distinguish, and the filled notebooks, where everything is meticulously recorded, are softened, the script is illegible. Writing goes on day by day, night by night although the damp paper absorbs the ink immediately. The years have gotten used to this, pile them up in a secret place, which they can no longer be found. The location constantly changes its position, and the years laugh about it, move onward, and know they are alive.

The night eaten

The night eaten, the day sliced in strips und wrapped around huge balls of fabric, a box full of buttons scattered in the landscape, afterwards spools of thread, hands clapped three times and then dipped in water, cracking sounds spun into skin, gestures abandoned in the air, the attendance certificates of missed moments issued, heartless stones expelled from the country, flattery heaped upon each hue, the light of the sun sucked in by the skin pores, got plastered, searched for the hand of the other, held, touched …

The matter is not straightforward

When we consider the situation, the matter is not straightforward. Admittedly, a goldfish is smaller than an octopus, but its inspiring impact is undisputed. If we deduct the value of the uncertainty principle and carefully detach it from this realization, a limited number of religious orientations arise as a result. If one adds to this the resulting cause of a randomly high exactness, we can all gain a mechanistic perspective from nature, which is potentially creative but simultaneously inexact. Viewed in this light, each perspective marks time and, in doing so, designs novel electronic circuits, which will only materialize in the future. If one takes this truly to heart and excludes any false use of conflicts, nothing stands in the way of movement toward an open glade.

Reconciliation

Because the insinuation can only lead to an unhappy ending, we create a tower out of the stacked wood, which projects into the sky, we collect the sea into a small bowl, where we dip our fingertips, scatter the ash of burnt maps onto our heads and smear them with our dampened fingertips on our faces, guide sun rays into our hearts and bundle them up, push forests and mountains ahead of us so in their exhaustion they finally find deep sleep, and can move on with us in the morning, burn the eyes of all photographs in the world so to reset them at any desired place and time, and we naturally tauten the sky, give it a coat of paint, and wait with the horizon for the reconciliation, which a young child pulls behind her on a string.

100 grams

The thought weighs 100 grams, which immediately slips
away and picks its nose in the corner there, drags finely
polished words into the light and throws them about. Theses
are skewered in a flash by triangular jokes, poured over with
melanin, a memento donned, which is dismantled and laid
on a bier in the meta-criticism of the post-embryonic state
with the assistance of the post-structural ramifications of the
postmodern, which closely relates to feudal constructivism
and its hunting party, which can promptly lead to iambic-
addicted architecture models, which have transatlantic
dimensions at their disposal, which in turn has a highly
probably transformation in virtual worlds as a consequence,
which ... and his thought does not progress any further, all
finely polished words lie in front of him in a heap of shards.
He climbs onto it, it crunches, and he walks on.

Authenticity's absence

First, the ribs of authenticity are cut out, its teeth are pulled
and hidden, its arms stuck into its trunk and rolled down
the street, across the meadows, through the forests, almost
drowned in the rivers, and finally in the sea its swimming
vest is donned. In the meantime, its lips purse into a crooked
smile, its eyes mist up for moments, before sounds thrust out
of its mouth, caught by its hands, and spread out, likewise
the penetrating looks, they must be collected, to distract
while hideous dwarves are made from giants, the sun torn
from the sky, the moon crumpled up and immediately dusted
with stars. Then it raises its eyes, squints in amazement, and
regrets its own absence.

Nothing but meaningless reincarnations

Nothing but meaningless reincarnations, which should give the world a new twist. On the contrary, they don't find their line under their chin, with which they softly draw or with appropriate rigor allow rooms to emerge. In lieu of this they swill blood with their eyes and ears, instead of using their mouth. Their arms hang down to the ground, they don't know what to do with them. One says to the other: you are dead. And the other nods its head until it falls off at the neck. And another looks around, and again, estimates the distance and ... years pass, caravans pass by inspired by fate and providence, which place drowned thoughts in their path, leading to collisions ... while the other has another go and jumps, reaches the earth's orbit, floats, and hopes to not be reincarnated again ...

The acquaintance

I have an acquaintance with luminous red eyes and a white mouth. She has three hands, four legs, but only one foot. Her nose lies across her face underneath her eye bags, her chin is magnificently rounded, her ears live at the back of her head, three pointed breasts and a thin belly, which my hand can encompass. Once a year she visits me with her animals: a three headed dog on one leg, which it balances on wonderfully, a tarantula which eats up my carpet, and a rabbit with teeth as sharp as razor blades, which always tears a steel cylinder, that my acquaintance prudently takes with her, to pieces for dessert. When she goes away with her animals, she leaves behind a battlefield, where I feel very uneasy until I have found a new apartment, where the acquaintance with her three animals visits me again—and it starts all over again.

The row of trees

That row of trees reminds me of yesterday. What I am trying to say is that to be able to walk in some direction, although no apparent connection exists and yesterday, I wasn't there yet. But I trust myself and scratch the colour from my skull, which, since I have been looking into the sun, persistently produces images. No rain in the process, no cold and wind. Everything stands still, no gesture distracts me, no sound, no pathological urge to put a word in my mouth.

Back then the temperature had found no fault with the cold, which lay under a stone—found no fault with the absent winds, which collected behind the forest on the horizon, and even when a sudden shower of hail broke the backbone of each blade of grass and coated them with ice, the temperature remained indifferent and did as if it hadn't seen a thing, and watched for me, only recognized the columns of air which distorted the view.

And I, completely discouraged, turn my head, press my chin into my chest; my ribs crack and break, which exasperates me, but I feel no pain and it occurs to me that promises made are to be kept, as this evening draws to an end, so I finally drop my gaze from the sun, fold it carefully, place it in my backpack, strap it on my shoulder and walk.

A night of broken pieces

Ultimately, and finally, absolutely, this humiliation with a
stiff collar and a cape full of holes. Burn marks on the ridge
of morning, stretched out between trees. And this wind
maintaining that wasted fields are dressed in lies, that the sky
is broken, but feels no pain, that the rough tree trunks protect
the midsummer day, that the light hides in the hay and the
remains of last night are kept in sight—this wind constantly
whispers and balances on the ridge of morning, climbs up
the cape, whistles through the holes and snaps the stiff collar
while the humiliation becomes less and less until it has
completely disappeared, and only the smell of burn marks
remains, dusted by light bursting forth from the hay. In the
background a night of broken pieces.

The cube

Carefully, so it doesn't break, he places his weight on the
grass, smoothens it and folds it into a cube. Then he climbs
up to the highest tip of the tree, holding tightly onto the
tree time and time again, otherwise he would fly away since
strong winds prevail up here. Sometimes he flutters like a
flag, pulling himself higher with his arms. Finally arrived,
he takes a seat on the end of the longest limb in the treetop,
bobs up and down until a gust of wind tears him away. At
first, he thinks he is floating, sees his cube in the grass below
becoming smaller and smaller, then the wind grabs and
drives him ahead.

The light pump

Evening laid his hands on the light pump and explained that
he would first provide sufficient pressure in the bicycle's inner
tube, would cross his arms and gingerly have to blow into
the face of the exhausted day, and be able to clearly convince
her that mounting a banner on her forehead was inevitable
for showing the way to the coming night; it's well known
that Night likes to take detours and then confuse everything
with its absence, and Evening is sorry he has to now cover
the light pump with his hand, since the night time is very
sensitive and at the slightest ray of light would immediately
go blind, which would certainly not be in the light pump's
interest, since he would then have to shatter her—and
Evening presses the light pump deeper and deeper into
his breast, swings himself onto the bicycle, which now had
plenty of air in the inner tube, and cycles towards Night.

To calm itself

To calm itself, a thought dissected its inflated hopes into
razor thin slices and painted them in conclusion with
abandoned rules of thumb, which it pulled from its dusty
perspective—and when it felt completely unobserved, the
thought rolled the slices to the surrounding coffee house
tables, which immediately jumped to the side and in doing
so tossed glasses and cups to the stone floor, where they
immediately shattered and produced a deafening clang—
since, as the thought determined, they had evidently not
learned otherwise, while it went in search of a bold forehead,
which would bring it shelter from the animosity of the world.

The transitions lack cues

The transitions lack cues. It's hard to believe with on average 1,000 double errors, always one of them blames the other. Even the sparse applause is not able to deter it, while the missing cues run up against the overall expectations, circle them and strangle them with bare hands. Emotionally speaking, this is a relief; from a moral perspective, however, one can only spit in disgust.

Next door the punishments hang on well-oiled hinges, while high above the rising moon with its unwavering dilatoriness convinces; its dull beam of light, which seeps into the darkness, and confuses the cues lying under the platform, lays a finely woven veil over everything and pays no heed to the transition's protest cries.

The street there

The street there rolls itself up and falls from the picture; the crow there on the tree branch, it pecks holes in the air with its beak; or the lonely woman at the window, she embraces the world, which slides from her parenthesis and threatens to fall onto the street. A rope extends across a river, sways, the reflection in the skylight breaks a thousandfold, loops the rope around the belly of the river flowing through the landscape, the street unfurls, washes it back into the picture again and fills the holes in the air with water: the river takes the lonely woman into its arms and flows with her from the world.

We all walked out into life

We all walked out into life. Each dressed in a white silk shirt
that reached to our thighs. Our figures were manicured, our
hair styled, each step tied into the other. We drove the days
ahead of us, sometimes we swung at them without soiling
ourselves. Now and then a ship came by, swelled its sails,
and demanded we climb aboard. But we ignored it, trusted
our steps. We didn't want to share the glory; we also had the
intention to provide our own income, step by step, with the
fluttering white shirt and manicured fingers. Sometimes we
stopped and looked at ourselves.

The rigid convictions

Of course, the rigid convictions throw themselves away, even
when most of them speak incoherently due to a lack of sleep.
They throw themselves at any stranger running along, you
are also included. They leech onto you and climb in networks
into your thoughts. It's warm in there, time plays no role,
and no entry fee is charged. The reception is magnificent,
each second one backdrop edges along after another so the
convictions are not bored. Light and shadows are not spared.
Well-trained thought habits in handcuffs and shackles
are paraded, fondled, beaten, maligned, only to please the
convictions now yawning, who stroke themselves satisfied
across their fat bellies.

Whoever this life

Whoever would like to turn in this life pays us only a small fee for the deleting of data from all registers. The lockers are fire and burglar-proof, each is equipped with a number combination, only for you. If you have additional wishes, we are available at any time for your inquiries. You will find in our catalogue thousands of pages of suggestions, which should make your stay more comfortable. Furthermore, we guarantee absolute quiet and no burdens. After your arrival spend two days in your locker, make yourself feel at home. We will subsequently sink you in the sea, bury you 1000 meters deep into the sea floor, pour concrete on top, and paint it with a camouflaged color. After all, you want to remain undetected. In comparison to other providers, we offer this last service free of charge.

Before your eyes

It would be more proper to not submit one single sentence and to ignore the official offers. Thus, the flattening of your skull, the furled chin and eyes covered with iron blinders. To play it safe you should glide along the veneered desktop, to the window, which opens the view into a garden.

A sharply curved palm shadow thrusts into the room and scrapes chalk from the walls. Grimaces hang from the ceiling in monomaniacal formats, remembering the earned faces of their last sentence architectures. They slowly come undone, dusted in chalk, which is still fluttering from the walls, and in one long forgotten corner of the room an official sentence in a menacing imbalance empties out a cardboard box where the rules of the tasker/ client wait for transformation, for your word which becomes a body. An afternoon passes thus; in your room the palm shadow has turned dull, and the iron blinders on your eyes turn to rust.

This certain thing

If you had had this certain thing, everything would have
been different, even the streets, which you could have
yanked from the landscape at any given time, artfully linked
together and wrapped around your forehead like a headband,
and you could have transfused the lake with the fish into
your waterglass, you could have folded up the horizon
and stretched and extended it from the next house corner,
running easily three times around the earth, swimming
through all seven seas, you would have befriended the fish
and the corals, could have been able to fly daily to different
continents, you would have made inventions, which would
serve humanity, would have had, would have been, could have
been, should have been, you would be, if you were allowed,
if you were, could have back then, if you had only had this
certain thing at the right time and place.

A curved glass cabinet

A curved glass cabinet always shines full of secrets while the movement of a carousel, the children sitting on it, a high wall in the background or a lost shelter, is something completely different. Just think about trouser pockets, stuffed full of casino chips, the sophisticated frescos of the Sistine Chapel, and the half dilapidated train station where conductors with gold wire-rimmed spectacles wander about, desperately searching for their trains, about the psychiatric assessment on your hand in a meditation phase before it shuts, and of course about a palatial outside staircase in its matinal throes; all of this is worth considering, is to be considered, and it occurs to me, have you ever given your hand over to a doubt, boozed through the night with it and in morning sat on suicide's bench next to the canal and puked.

My friends…

My friends and comrades, right and left, top and bottom, are exasperated. I get it, all their aide-de-camps and sycophants have summarily resigned without explaining why. This stoppage, of course, will hamper the development of any personality, render it toothless, shake it with ominous fright, and leave it to wander the world with glum looks. And then, occasionally, they cross right through me, or I walk with them part of the way before they let go again and return to their time-tested places of solace. And if it wasn't for the memories coming, they'd bury themselves there, pour themselves full of concrete, and offer themselves up as monuments.

But every time I approach them with open arms, in winter, spring, autumn, summer, on rainy days, and during droughts, and when I accidentally break into their false places of solace, the sun falls from their eyes.

Wire entanglement

The wire entanglement writes a letter complaining about not being allowed to move, having to stay put in the same place, for all seasons. Freezing in winter, sweating under the blazing summer sun, no shadows, no one to talk to. Without ever having seen the world. And, no provisions are sent, not even some soup or bread. He worries about his vocabulary thinning out because of isolation, while everything around him is in motion. Even though women, children, and men get caught up in it, ripping their bodies open, it is impossible to engage in conversation with them. Instead, he ducks under a hail of bullets, steady shelling, and the guns, whips, and clubs of the guards.

In this letter, the wire entanglement demands, in no uncertain terms, strict adherence to the chain of command, threatens to file a report with his immediate superiors, and applies for home leave, as his sense of loneliness and isolation is growing by the day. He has become a security risk.

Legs and arms

Legs and Arms are carefully folded down to the size of fists, sealed with cellophane, and placed on the designated shelves. There's nothing to indicate persecution, pillage, or slander. Passers-by say their polite hellos and automatically fumble for their legs and arms. This used to happen to us at times, too; we remember the pleasure of stroking thighs, and arms, those were moments of submission.

Today, however, we sit in the front behind the checkout counter, slide fist-sized cellophane balls across the scanner before holding out our hands. We sometimes feel dejected over the fact that in any given year, only two or three customers will stray into our premises, and once they realize what they are about to buy and where they are, we must forcefully coax them into closing the deal.

Storm of rays

There was only a grove, pale light from all sides. Not a
trace was left, aside from the green light shimmering out
from under the rock in the clearing. A group of men and
women were standing in a trench, smiling at the sky that was
gathering storm clouds and smothering the sun.

One of the men bent down and pulled the green light out
from under the rock, folded it and put it in his backpack,
which he slung over his shoulders. The others paid no mind
to him, but were busy confabulating, touching themselves
and each other with their hands, caressing them, while the
guy with the green light in his backpack jumped out of
the trench and left the clearing—walked across fields and
meadows, stopping now and then to look back towards the
clearing, waving to the women and men who had opened
their umbrellas in the trench, trying to attract lightning from
the sky with their iron tips. They stood naked in a storm of
rays—that glaringly lit up the earth and the sky.

The background in the foreground

Let me repeat, in the background, behind the sycamore tree, the foreground was green, and he presented himself, in accordance with his assignment, in a blonde wig and black swim shorts, standing straight as an arrow and puffing his chest, as the background in the foreground of the sycamore tree tugged at and tickled the lower right edge of the foreground behind the sycamore tree, or, more precisely, three meters and thirty centimeters, to remind him to get out of the picture, and the fact that the green foreground did not burst into sardonic laughter can be chalked up to coincidence; instead, he straightened himself, puffed out his chest even further and casually leaned against the sycamore tree, thus trying to completely obliterate the view of the background who screamed in protest at this show of defiance, but didn't know what to do next, collapsed in on himself, cloaked himself in a black cloud and successively assumed all visible colors—but when this was of no avail either, the infuriated background stole out of the picture to try his luck elsewhere, while the foreground cracked an embarrassed smile, as the blond wig had slipped from his bald head and left it glistening in the sun.

Fish

Fish run the flywheel of time, which needs to remain a secret. They swim the waters, belly up, hang on to fishhooks, disguised as tourists they invade our cities, others dive to the bottom of the sea, sling grappling hooks into the rocks, wriggle in nets beneath the surface or pass their time with heated discussions about the meaning of life and waste management.

They let themselves be killed, gutted, filleted, roasted, or steamed without raising any objections. Their bones pierce tongues, get jammed between teeth and stuck in throats. But their eyes, their eyes are legendary, they see everything all the way to the very end, and beyond. That's why they run the flywheel of time.

Bodies on the water

These bodies on the water, gently flickering images in the sun, are wet planes, weary from flying over mountain ranges of remembrance, over their deserts and valleys and jungles. These bodies carry with them the fruit of their actions, which gradually dissolve in the water. They bear with them their friendships with scorpions and snakes as they float away down the river.

One of the bodies sinks to the bottom of the river, wearily descending towards all that has been lost, which has been awaiting it there for centuries. The other bodies slightly move their hands and fingers, caressing the frigid waters and spreading their arms, breathing in and filling their lungs with the scent of the waves, growing empty, afloat on the current—and the river rolls and rolls and rolls.

The young twigs

The young twigs fell from the trees onto the nursery rhymes, covering and tickling them, while two legs ran around town, beneath the sky that had turned into a billboard. Children played with balls, covered their mouths with both hands, and kicked their glances into the languid flow of the river. The flowers along the shore tugged their hair, shook dust and bees from their calyxes.

Just then a strange sound crept up from the bushes, jumped on the two legs and raced them to the young twigs outside the city limits, lifted them carefully and crawled to the nursery rhymes. It was all cheers and laughter. Elephants, tigers, and polar bears joined their company, a patch of sky, a cup of sea, a shard of moon, a bit of sun.

Electric shocks

In this case, bitter alkaloids are administered first, which cause a strong mouth odor. It's then reasonable to demand the immediate removal of such persons and the annulment of their human rights, which would only complicate matters. In case they refuse immediate removal and throw emptiness, or, what's even scarier, all their weight around, they need to be smothered with stardust.

You can, of course, also bring their white blood cells into a state of excitation by means of electric shocks, which causes the blood to boil throughout the body and leads to a shift in the position of the limbs. We should keep in mind, of course, that the horror that occurs in the process must be torn out at the root at an earlier point.

They just sit there

They just sit there, next to each other, and the spirits of combat bite the dust at their feet. No betrayal had occurred, but still. With the requisite sternness of rivals, the steps are moved, chasms are refined. Threads are crisscrossed and tightened to cushion the weight of the burden of debt. A ledge is carried in with inhuman effort and stamina, vows are renewed, and certainties thrown into a heap, pushed to the left, to the right, a little upwards, then downwards. The threads stretch, break, while chocolates are stuffed into all exits and entrances.

Beginner and advanced skills

While beginners are limited to undoing the brightness excesses of shades of black in the details, the drawing of the moon remains true to itself. The reign and mysterious charm of nature rarely disentangle themselves from the embrace, and it's more prudent to step into the human brain, take a walk, and return in a daze. Most of the time, the flavors of the month then include breathlessness, ideas for a senseless murder, or a stringent definition of the universe, which, as an apple seed, lies in the palm of your hand.

By contrast, more advanced skills contribute to the cooling of our planet, help divert the effects of all pollutants and sell them for profit. Many of them sail the seas and continents with solar sails and often take time out to clear rainforests, drive deserts inland, let rivers run dry, or drink them up, and wage wars designed to fertilize the world with their dead.

Water running from your ears

See the window, the glass, the dried putty, close it and step out into the street, drag your memory across the asphalt, which causes it to glow from the friction, to soften, to move in ripples and waves, while your suitcase stands on the other side of the street, filled with water, impatient, between two passers-by, statues made of loam, and they push towards you, reaching out for you with their hands, but you keep on walking. Water runs from your ears, your mouth, your nose, your eyes. They show first cracks, you stretch out your hands in front of you so as not to bump in to things, you ride waves, sway up and down, smell the sweating asphalt, the hot air clings to your lungs, and you ride, up and down, in circles, faster and faster, until you stumble and fall over your suitcase, open it, swill down its water, drink yourself senseless.

The proof

The proof of God's existence has yielded the formula: sleep plus soul times gesture to the power of chance. Which leads us to the realization that the squeaky iron hinges of the front door need to be oiled, three or four drops of sewing machine oil will do, and that this front door has nothing whatsoever to do with the drop in sea levels or paint that won't dry— there is thus ample proof of God's existence despite all the official denials.

We simply must accept that a squeaky door is an issue that can arise at any moment, and, at the same time, we would like to point to the fact that at any given time, there's always room to choose the wrong time. The ensuing unit of measurement is something we are still working on. Yet, its proper application remains a mystery. But we're not giving up.

A handful of sand

A handful of sand understands what it's all about here on this earth. Does it not? Every day, each grain of sand hatches into a new shape. That's why the world is crowded with so many people. Distilleries, computer terminals, and various other critters are springing up all over the place. Lions remain excluded, and the same goes for the angels who were expelled from the country for good in the wake of a recent board meeting.

Inconspicuous as a grain of sand may be, its powers of self-assertion and perseverance are immense. Yesterday, for example, the slender shadow of a cloud moved across the hills, along with a magnificent snow pattern, as the snow's been melting for days now. And the grain of sand made no attempt to sugarcoat or clear anything away; imagine that: it left everything entirely to itself, free of any interpretation. A superior mindset indeed!

Columns of displaced persons

Again, an unnatural stillness, only the growing of ivy on the wall, a rustle at long intervals, a barely perceptible change of the shadow. Often, days passed as we waited for the next soft crackling of the ivy, as if it was stretching and rubbing its delicate knuckles together, while columns of displaced persons incessantly passed in front of the courtyard, women, men, and children who joined us in the yard and listened to the growing of ivy, who ate our soups, bread, lard, and apples, drank our freshly squeezed elderberry juice.

Then they left again, joined the columns of displaced persons outside. No scuffling of feet on the floor, no rustling of clothes, no voices, as if they were figments of the imagination without sound, and from time to time we leaned close to each other, briefly looking into each other's eyes, touching each other before turning our heads back to the ivy, listening, while the columns of displaced persons passed by our house.

Saved-up eternity

Not love between the planets, which is becoming ever more obscene, disrupts our meeting, but all the saved up eternity that you will find in every nook and cranny around here. Her life is driven by enthusiasm, she deciphers all the runes, reads the footprints of the night, coalesces with the day, with anyone, if need be. She delights in pressing herself against steamed up glass in winter or squeezes in between car tire threads. She seizes on every movement, every rotation.

And when the horizon flutters, one word from her is enough and it's gone. When the sea begins to self-harm out of feelings of inferiority—it likes to cut deep wounds—saved up eternity is on the scene, twine and thread at the ready, and sutures the wound. When we humans reach for a glass to drink, for example, we can rest assured that it will take a sip first; if we kiss a woman for the first time, it has done so long before us. We can communicate in coded languages, but she's known all along what we have to say.

One fine day

When, one fine day, everything is over, your ruin curled up under dainty wings and the lid slammed shut on your self-development, no darkness, no summer lightning will have the power to overcome you. The birds will fall from the trees, the grass and the wind will pass by in silence, your voices will become one, the suns will light up the corners of your eyes and the sky will sink deeper into the universe, casually, and carry you on its broad shoulders, while your heart ignites in your chest, casting dancing shadows on the horizons to come.

A promising start

The wet traces on the azure flannel were promising. Next, the windowpanes trembled from a passing truck, a forgotten stiff frozen coat in a field of snow in front of the house, the deleted totals in the cashbook that lay on the kitchen table beneath so many white tiles. But it was no use.

The register of actions was posted in the hall, a wide river of slush rolling through it, piling up against the room doors, almost up to the ceiling. On top of that, an unexpected lunar eclipse diverted attention from the scene. Somewhere someone coughed, which certainly did not lead to any results. The undulating landscape began to show minor oddities and declared itself ready to receive new instructions.

Meanwhile, the wet traces on the azure flannel were drying. The moon is still gone, and now the stiff frozen coat rises from the snow and trudges across the field. Once more, somewhere someone coughe d. With this we rest our case and will keep it on file.

Reconciliation with rocks

Reconciliation with the rocks is showing signs of progress.
One floor below, two arms embrace a tree. A face leans
against the bark, ears listening into the depths of space,
which revolves around itself like a paddle wheel. It is
impervious to smells. It produces deserts and lush forests,
rivers and seas, and turns, paddle wheeling, shouldering
rocks and whirling them into the air, juggling them, and
writing into the wind with them the sum of all angles—and
prostrating itself with them before the light.

Drink the flesh

Drink the flesh, together with the bones, chew the water,
the milk, and anoint yourself with sifted earth, your eyes and
tongue as well, and drink and chew, rest in yourself, go for a
run through the air, circle the tops of trees, chew their tender
buds and run on, keep being yourself and spread your arms to
embrace the world.

In reality

There's a young man inside reality. That's highly credible. The young woman over there is also inside reality—why not believe that? Reality undulates slightly upwards at its ends, which causes many people to stay inside its confines, whether they like it or not—or because they are too lazy and fearful to step beyond boundaries.

Some realities are made to measure. Tall people usually prefer spacious ones, so as not to bump into things everywhere all the time. Little people tend to favor the small and manageable ones; they come with the advantage of being able to merge with larger realities, of joining into one in a discreet manner.

But experience has shown that big and large ones can connect, as well. Yesterday we saw a satellite image of the earth—billions of realities, of rolling fields of rapturous grass.

Climb higher

Climb higher, take your hands out of your pockets, you'll need them to pray to the setting sun. You're still dragging behind you the faith in yesterday, its blood choking the water veins, becoming encrusted. High above, the eagle is silently winging its way, the chapel its eye, with all its turbines and dynamos, in between its broken axle and the healing spring. You must reach it, pull the ladder out of your pain, lean it against the rock walls, climb higher, don't get confused because it's nighttime, and you'll sink knee-deep into the rock with every step you take. Don't stop, it has nothing to do with you, just climb higher, towards the light.

The first night

Praise be to the aborted journeys inside those houses,
the wake trails on their oceans, the precious seed on the
foreheads of lovers, the rumpled bed, bare feet on the
wooden floor, shouldering the charge of the previous night,
the warm milk in the glass, on your tongue—and the trail of
drops on your lips, your chest, emerging from the being that
rises in every body like bread.

You sleepy child

Arms folded in lap. It's better that way, and then, later,
the dream and trees swaying in the wind. They carve their
messages into the windowpanes; birds fall from the sky. And
one of them will slip into your heart, will build his nest there,
will bathe in your blood, balance on your veins at night,
launch into a chirping competition with your long forgotten
words and await the morning, night after night, and you're
going to think that it's the tide of your blood that makes your
body resonate, all through your life, you sleepy child.

from *In the Rhythm of Spaces*

The Morning

The morning has been lying in a prone position for days, surrounded by fish washed up from the rivers. Giggling mischievously under their hats and tickling their beards, they slap their tails across the face of the morning. Their loud clapping makes the trees move closer together and think of fleeing. The fish remain unimpressed, chattering on, tearing at their whiskers, and finally rolling onto the belly of the morning. Their translucent scales and golden-gleaming bones encase a beating heart the size of an almond pit. A night cut short flows by and issues its blessing to the surrounding fields. For a moment the fish turn silent, and soon, they line up, holding their beards into the rising air currents. Their hearts are whirled and tossed around inside their bone cages, the wind strengthens into a storm that swirls the fish from the belly of the morning, and with that it is able to rise and open its spaces.

Too Late

Probably the photograph would not have been mistaken for the wilted flowers on the windowsill, nor confused with the dirty curtains, if everyone had stuck to the plan. Quickly grabbing the umbrella would have sufficed to settle the question of ownership, throw in a little patience for good measure—and no one would have gotten wet.

But at that point it was already too late to get any meaningful action started. The road was in place, three flights of stairs were swept, two rivers diverted, and the sea had been carted in from the Far East. No one looked up to parse the photograph in more detail, saw then that it was attached with two clothespins to a string, with the windowsill and the wilted flowers in the background. The air was calm, two clouds pushed over each other, and the blue sky turned red. The photograph was drying in the sun, birds perched on a scarecrow in a nearby field where the umbrella lay in the grass, unopened. A shadow circled the photograph, which had come loose from a clothespin, as a heavy rain began to fall. We rushed to take shelter under the eaves of a roof, the umbrella still lying in the field, along with the photograph and the windowsill with the wilted flowers. We should have intervened right away, and while we were mulling doing so, the windowsill with the wilted flowers, the photograph, and the umbrella began to fade. We had to close our eyes, or they would have been washed out by the rain.

First Meeting

As the shadows are driven through the spring corridor, they lose their rigid shape: arms, legs, and head become one with the upper body, before the shadows dissolve altogether. All they leave behind are their shirts with wet spots under the armpits that slowly dry in the sun. A baby carriage rolls by, its wheel suspensions squeaking, twigs, leaves swirl through the air and a carpet of clouds covers the park. Just now, two birds are shedding their first drops of sweat this morning, a third is emerging from the eggshells of sleep, and a fourth is hanging its plumage out on a branch to air it out. Birdsong fills the park, the baby carriage wheels continue to squeak, the white shirts of shadows gleam in the sun, and the birds sit down for their first meeting with the day.

An environment

We live in an environment that is constantly changing. Some days the sun rises in the south, and in the north on others, only coming out at midnight when everyone's asleep. Because for years, everyone's been tucked into their sleeping bags in the early evening, zippered up over their heads, soft music playing while a sleep-inducing drug is administered intravenously. That's why most only know the sun from school textbooks. Other visual material is banned.

In the old days there were gardens, meadows, forests, rivers, lakes, and oceans, all in perpetual motion. Today, everything has dried up, the hills and mountains have turned barren. It's strange to wander this terrain. Huge canvases rise to the left and right of the path, painted with forests, houses with gardens, entire villages surrounded by fields and pastures, where cows graze and children play. Or, destroyed, abandoned towns appear out of nowhere—and because their sight is unbearable, dense snowfall commences; it is blasted into the countryside from giant blowers, and everything is submerged in an undulating white blanket of snow. Or a sea of flames eats through the screen, exploding the houses of towns. The smell of burnt wood and molten iron fills the air, crunching, cracking, and roaring sounds all around, the earth trembles, just as it did back when nights were just a blur, days had a tight grip on us, and it had become impossible to take a single step without falling to the ground. That's when we learned to stay put, lying, sitting, standing still, getting by for years without the sun, while a sea of flames continued to eat away at the screen, brightly lighting up the sky.

These dreams

These dreams have undergone a fundamental change. Any orientation in time and space is gone, allocated spaces switch their locations, steal corners from their peers, and step on each other's toes. That keeps them busy for hours, with the suits faction pressing forward, forever adjusting the knots of their ties, first with one hand, then with the other, while they still find time to indecently assault the other spaces. Or they strap their ties around their hips, or thighs, stuff them into their chests, where the heart sits, crack dirty jokes, crumple up other spaces and just leave them lying around, take their heads off their shoulders, fling them high into the air and start juggling them. After three minutes flat, everyone gets their head back. A strict choreography prevails: now, spaces begin to touch, deform, and repel each other. There are thousands with not a whisper of wind inside them, as if they were holding their breath.

In the shadow of the dream

In the shadow of the dream, he sets out to take action, wraps a desert round his waist, as a loincloth, sticks tongue-moistened flower petals into the air, and, from the temple remnants that suddenly appear, he takes a column, solemnly carries it into the mountains, and erects it in a gorge. He circles the pillar, slides his right hand under it and lifts it up, while tearing the encroaching sky asunder with his teeth, with all its stars, which softly rain down on the flower petals in the air. Just then a wind rounds the corner, the sound of a drum is heard in the distance, high above the gorge the bursting of glass, and, as he takes a step to the side to get out of harm's way, he falls and falls and hits the hardwood floor, right next to his bed, where the dream was pulling the covers over his head.

The Folding Pattern

The patterns on your forehead are reminiscent of folded hands. I know, that's a contrived way of looking at it, almost as if from the current position of your eyes under those bushy eyebrows, where insects get entangled every day and try to settle in, despite the steep incline of your head. It sits on too small a neck, one with no tendons protruding, with only pale skin, taut to the point of tearing. It contrasts with your face, which looks like a jagged rock landscape that's always in motion: the furrows around your slanted mouth push into each other, deepen into your skin, overlap, crack at the surface, and peter out on your cheeks, while two deep wrinkles race down from your nose when your mouth strains to smile.

You don't have to put on an act, you've forgotten how to even things out where it's necessary. Just yield to the play of free forces, be happy about the ongoing population of your eyebrows, the ever-changing color of your eyes, your wrinkles, and the mesh of shades that covers your face. There are bright sides to this, for instance the folded hands on your forehead that now begin to open.

Oh, the crackling

First, the word is flayed, and its skin is stretched out between steel posts embedded in the ground, the sun is dimmed down to the lowest level, and the air currents are diverted, the skinned word would otherwise be blown away. There's not a breath of wind. The outside temperature is lowered until fine ice needles protrude from the edges of the taut skins, like hairs bristling from a thin pelt. Humidity is held constant to keep the skins from drying and cracking.

In the meantime, the skinned word disintegrates into its component parts: letter by letter, rearranged into new sequences. All its characters bask in their nudity and new-found possibilities. Some pamper themselves, rubbing earth and grass on their bodies, gathering berries, and getting drunk on their juice, while discovering unexpected talents in other members of the alphabet. This strengthens their sense of community!

When darkness falls, they all reassemble to form the word again. Under the cover of the word, things are easier, even though it has gotten cold and it's hard to breathe. Without making a sound, the word reaches for the steel posts and grabs the skin, still hemmed with bristles of ice, unfastens it and wraps it around all its letters. With every move, ice needles sprinkle to the ground, like snow, the word thinks, as it lies in a bed of crackling needles and feels the letters comfortably stretching out on its inside.

Inlays

Work on brain inlays is progressing by leaps and bounds.
Before they are finally inserted, they are plated with gold
and trimmed until they fit into even the smallest folds and
crevices of the brain. In the process, some of the existing
tissue structure needs to be modified, holes are drilled, access
routes are created, and some areas require planing. We throw
the ensuing shavings into the red-hot furnace next to the
hall entrance. When we raise ourselves up again, we see our
dead, who have occupied every sofa and armchair in the hall.
They wink at us, pull their ears, because they're seated where
we would like to be sitting once our work is done—with
exquisite food, wine, and the women and men we have hired
in town.

Without putting up any resistance, our dead let us lock them
back into their cellars, and we would have surely enjoyed
another happy evening if it hadn't been for the open shutters
that the storm raging outside banged against the house wall
like crazy, causing the house and the parquet floor to tremble
and all the brain inlays to come loose, fall to the floor, and
shatter.

That made us forget all about the women and our empty
stomachs—we knelt and gazed at the splinters, unaware that
our dead had returned from the cellars and had laid their
hands on our heads to comfort us.

Found turns of words

Found turns of words are nothing to speak of compared with the body parts of the cuckoo, which, as is commonly known, is named after the cuckooflower. Folksy reinterpretations are out of the question, forget about planting flower spores in bird crests. The same goes for all the cuckoo crazies, cuckoo's eggs, and cuckolds that populate the ever-fallow realms of double meanings. Incidentally, the crop rotation economy is not what it used to be either. Right now, the severed spores bashfully leave town, in search of new metaphorical employment. Even though a botanical usage referencing past events is envisaged, the endeavor is in an early stage of development and already overgrown with lichens and grasses. The first among our ranks begin to despair and contemplate suicide, since all of this is taking too long.

It's best we quickly forget all that's happened and turn to other evidence, interpretations that turn every verb into an adjective and vice versa, plus one or two tighter plot threads with players who must be re-selected before they're thrust back into their own entanglements and overwhelmed by verbs and adjectives. Folksy reinterpretations are out of the question.

You've Cried Enough

You've cried enough. Hang your blue hat on a nail in the door. Autumn is here again. The years brush against you, want to wash you away, and flow by, pulling strings in their wake. It's okay for you to jump over them without touching them. You succeed in doing just that. During the big breaks, you drink your cup of hot chocolate, standing under the huge window in the event hall.

A random passerby plays your little brother and asks in amazement: "So this is the school you're going to?" And he gifts you two marbles and his blue cap. The ceremoniousness of it all! Keep calm and slip it into your coat pocket. Your little brother wipes the tears from your cheeks as he says goodbye, smiling. As you gaze after him, you feel the two marbles in your pocket and the rough fabric of his cap in your hands.

But then you get entangled in the strings of years past that you can no longer jump because you're just too tired, because they wrap you up in sheets and drag you out of the hall, through the aisles, and into the courtyard. There, shoes stomp on your stomach, your head is kicked around like a soccer ball. They'll let you crawl a bit. By all means, pay no attention to the stream of blood shooting from your nose, that would hold you back, and don't be surprised that the kicks are concentrated on your chest and legs and ... suddenly your little brother bends over you, he has aged, and someone next to you says, "She is already dead, too." Just let them talk.

When He Wanted to Get Up

When he wanted to get up, he noticed he had lost his legs, and when he wanted to support himself with his hands on the table, he realized his arms had vanished. When he shouted for the innkeeper to order something to eat, he couldn't utter a sound, all was silent, and then he saw the knife stuck in his chest, the blood soaking his white shirt, but he didn't feel any pain, was completely numb, even though at that moment an axe plunged into his back, a hand covered his eyes, and when it was pulled back out, he could no longer see anything, felt only the gaping wound in his back, and all that wouldn't have been so bad, he could have gotten used to it, even to losing his sense of smell. But the fact that the innkeeper simply walked past him, coins jingling in his pockets, clucking his tongue, scratching his chin, and launched into a lively conversation with some empty tables in the dining area, that was the most unbearable thing he had ever experienced.

At the Head of the Mattress

All the valuable things we have collected over the course
of the rainy season are stored at the head of the mattress.
A dripping branch, hollowed apples, washed up hands,
limp, emaciated bodies dozing away in the waterside mud.
Strikingly, they are carefully combed. Their skin is bloated,
their bellies look as if they were pregnant. Legs spread
wide—ready for the birth canal to open. But nothing ever
comes out of their wide-open mouths—not a sound!

Snakes slither across their foreheads, spiders build webs in
their hands, catch sunlight, wrap it in silk, and place it on the
bloated bellies at the shore. Against the light, the tide rises,
washes away the bodies and carries them away. High in the
sky, birds pick out the stars with their beaks.

We're still lying on our mattress at the shore, snorting like
horses about having survived. As we try to sleep, blinking out
at the sea, the tide has come in again, pulling the mattress
and us into the darkness.

My Country's Horizon

After I have carefully folded the country in which I have
lived since my birth, and packed it in the paper bag, I let
water run in my bathtub and take a bath, wash the spaces
between my toes thoroughly, two or three times, scrub my
belly with a brush and smear cream on my skin so it stays
supple. Then I take out my left eye, let it roll in the palm of
my hand, smoothen it with fine sandpaper I got in the city
yesterday, and press the eye back into my socket. The result is
extraordinary—I can now discern the rusty water pipes and
electric cables in the walls. The sight of this depresses me.
Through the closed bathroom door, I see my paper bag on
the kitchen sideboard, where my country is trying to unfold.
The paper bag wavers, trembles, menacingly tilts forward,
threatening to fall from the sideboard to the tiled floor. The
impact on the contents of the bag on my country would
be unimaginable. I want to take my country around in my
garden for half an hour, so it sees, smells, tastes something
different once and for all, not just itself. I'll take my country
carefully out of the paper bag and lay it in the moss in front
of the apple tree. The sun's already shining, its rays will warm
my country and I'll stand in front of it, to give it shade if
necessary.

Then it occurs to me: my country's horizon, its delicate fabric,
how should I spread it out without tearing it, and a country
without a horizon, that's no good. I jump out of the bathtub
to rescue what can still be rescued, slip on my bathrobe, run
to the kitchen sideboard, and reach for the paper bag. Right
after my first step I notice I must hold it at a certain angle,
otherwise my country might run out.

I carefully put down the paper bag, jump to the wardrobe, take out my bathing trunks and put them on. I don't need any more than this as I'll just be in my garden surrounded by high cypress perennials. As I reach to lift up the paper bag, it is no longer there, just a moist spot on the floor, and I consider whether to jump into it, after all I am wearing my bathing trunks. It's the least I can do for my country.

The Shadows

But the shadows did stay, after all, on the piece of wood that the river had washed ashore, albeit only for a short while. They ducked and sniffed at the wood to which algae clung like thick tangled hair. They cautiously climbed down to the ground and up the embankment, feeling fragile, knowing that their blood had become watery, and their kidneys were left with nothing to do, and they had to get ready to die.

Then a dead man, whimpering, with a knife in his chest, stood in their path and revealed the name of his murderer, the details of the circumstances, and what may have motivated him, and that he himself may have been to blame for his murder, that he had downright longed for it, and there was no end to the sobs, it was pretty unbearable, but in a strange way it loosened the shadows' limbs. Their blood thickened until their kidneys worked at full stretch again and, without a word, the shadows descended to the piece of wood on the shore, sat down on it—shadows can absorb thousands of others—reached the middle of the river and glided right into the heart of the night.

Death Has Long Been Intruding

Death intrudes into my burial chamber where he binds a
wreath of litanies, plucks twigs from them and sticks them
into my hair. He spins like a dervish, he steams, he sweats,
he slams against the walls of my tomb; with his frantic dance
he paints my life onto the rocks, he crosses out, he inserts,
he sits with me, his sweat drips into my eyes and seals them
shut. As I offer no resistance, he jumps to his feet, stretches
himself, rolls the stones from the entrance, rejoices and
runs out of my burial chamber and into the night, clambers
up and down, dances prayers into the darkness, and dives
headlong into the light of the coming day—he wanders from
budding births, which he wraps in white linen sheets, to
dying men, wiping the sweat from their brows, thus renewing
the alphabet of his presence, tenderly stroking weary faces,
bedding them in his warm lap, and winking at them in
encouragement.

The Breath Slinger

The breath slinger has been shut down due to outstanding payments. The owner has neither carried out required maintenance nor brought it in for service on the scheduled dates, where fine-tuning would have extended its service life. As of today, the grace period has expired and the braces and struts inside the oral cavity as well as filters installed around the exit of the trachea must be dismantled, along with the suction tubes attached to the palate. While this will severely compromise voice transmission, there are no feasible alternative options: it is already in no condition to render gestures or regulate the raising and lowering of the smallest volumes of air that are responsible for vibrations in the voice. Likewise, it is no longer capable of generating tremors in the air and the most subtle breaths of wind, which give to it its very own sound, its rhythm, and are intrinsic to every spoken word. It's hard to feel unaffected by the pity of it all, but we can't let ourselves be distracted and need to unmount the last support systems.

The gargling of the voice slowly dies down, the last breath of air leaves the lungs and wafts out from the mouth. We then seal the trachea and, after thorough disinfection and cleaning, pack up the struts and parts of the air filter that are suitable for refurbishment and future reuse, together with the signed and stamped forms confirming the dying off of the voice and the concurrent failure of all organs.

Cross-Stitches

Birds circling inside the cloud crater cast their lines and glide down to earth with the first rays of light. The journey is long and dangerous due to air turbulence, chasms, and downdrafts, and then there's also the sewing machine in the sky that is stitching seams around the edges of the clouds. She doesn't know why she has to do that. She loves the rattle of her needles, her well-aimed stabs—and doesn't care whether her needle is stitching flesh or water vapor. Sometimes a bird falls to earth, ruffled, with its breast torn open, a thread hanging from a gaping wound.

At night, with no clouds at hand, the sewing machine has tried to thread birds on a string. Only a few venerable, old birds allowed themselves to be blindsided, while the young ones proved too agile, swooping through the air, soaring, circling near and far, flying loops, taunting the machine that rattled obtusely across the sky, stitching into the air, piercing whatever came under her needle. This is why today the air is littered with cross-stitches and the sewing machine keeps clattering across the sky. Can you hear it?

In the Morning

Will the morning trees carry the echoes of the previous night on into the day? Will the wind bow down at the sight of the day, who is leaning asleep against the rock face, freshen him up and take him by the hand? Will this dome pushing into our view be that of a Sunday or Monday or some other day? And will it really be important to see the sky, the horizon, the previous night, or just our next steps on the stairs that rise in every direction inside the body of the day?

Some of these stairways reach the river, where birds weave an invisible carpet with their song and lay it on the landscape, others, in turn, lead into gardens where the night still hangs in the branches while the day rubs the sleep from his eyes.

The Empty Space

Too little attention is paid to the empty space in our thinking. It's mostly hidden away in the furthest corners of our consciousness; its existence is denied and fenced in with barbed wire, while snatches of sound are released into the air and words are piled into heaps and distributed generously. Anyone passing by is given a chain of words, which is tightly strapped around their neck, and a second one is used to flog them and march them off. They stagger across furrowed fields, divert rivers, without looking up, because they're following orders, all caught up in themselves, in the motion of moving forward, caught up in the pain of cracked skin because they're following orders. Through all of this, it never occurs to them that they keep walking the same routes, dodging the blows of the word chains of strangers to produce piles of their own words. They focus on putting one foot in front of the other—while imagining themselves gracefully sashaying into the world.

At every turn, they must confirm to themselves that they exist, even when already entangled in the barbed wire enclosing their empty space. Then, moments of silence fall and their gaze loses itself in the confined void.

The Body Fans Out

The body fans out into the distance, takes to its heels, sneaks up on openings, establishes boundaries, and draws lines that parallel the sky. Your hair catches fire, a hand reaches deep into your chest and unlocks its channels. Your chin reminds of an abandoned office and the ideas you have forgotten mop the linoleum floor. But the distance, it has waited, it douses the flames and indicates your exact location, to initiate the ritual of departure: sounds of gargling and panting subside into silence, avoid eye contact, and undress as they drift into a flight that takes you away. Down below, there in the distance, lies your flesh with its shallows, depths, and protocols of your life, it is flotsam on the long road out of this world.

Part of the Protocol

The protocol includes a brawl between two men hanging from nails hammered into the air, wildly flailing their arms, and kicking each other. Their eyes roll in their sockets, mouths clenched, then agape, contorted. This has been going on for an hour, and, in the meantime, the nearby public swimming pool has opened. The woman next door, who's watching the men dangling from nails through the ironing room window, pours herself a cup of coffee and leans against the windowsill; still drowsy with sleep, the garden wall squints at the morning sun and glances at the shallow layer of fog hovering above the treetops. Some distance away, a man kisses his wife, whom he will cheat on today with his lover in a hotel room, a group of kids runs across the street to the bus stop, laughing and scuffling until the bus stops right in front of them. The first shops open around the swimming pool area, the woman next door puts her empty cup in the sink, the garden wall straightens up and casts a long shadow across the tarmac, the fog dissipates in the morning sun that blinds the man who, by tonight, will have cheated on his wife with his lover and will get into a heated argument with her, drink himself into a stupor, and sleep outside the front door of his house.

Undeterred, the next hour rolls around, amused by the men now dangling limp from their nails, looking around and becoming aware of the morning bustle around them, who pays no heed to them and has put up a plexiglass wall that prevents any noise from getting through to them. He intends to write in peace, needs to get an overview of all the storylines, and when he pauses briefly and looks around, he notices the two men on their nails, the look of despair in their faces, their strength drained from them; they can neither speak nor scream nor raise a fist, all they hear is their own breath, which fills them with fear. Both begin to sob. The next hour makes its thunderous arrival. A child buys a popsicle at the pool, the woman next door starts to read a book, the garden wall leans forward to get a better view of the man, who will have cheated on his wife by evening, as he walks with stiff steps toward the bus stop.

Just This Handful of Things

I place on the bed just this handful of things: the tattered book, its pages yellowed over the years, the oval stone that has lodged in my head since childhood, which I warm during the day and pull out of my head in the evening, so that it at least gets enough air at night; then, the withered rose whose leaves rustle ever so delightfully with every breath I take, because it's lying on my chest. I don't know why I picked it up, but I solemnly carry it around the apartment before I go to sleep, bed it right next to the letter I started writing years ago, which is covered with coffee stains and kept alive by my deletions; and not forgetting the broom that I put at the end of my bed, which will sweep me into my sleep. Under the bed I put the crutches and pulleys that keep me upright during the day and provide my body with the necessary tension.

But before I finally go to bed, I have to look out into the unlit courtyard, say good bye to the shadows that flit about between the equipment of the children's playground, restlessly, all through the night; and it's only then that I can go to bed, surrounded by things dear to me, and excitedly await the moment when I am finally swept into my sleep.

The Thought

Right from the start, the thought moved at a wrong angle to the room—too shallow, too indecisive. It bounced off again and again and had to rearrange itself before giving it another try. In the meantime, remnants of foreign words slid past it like shooting stars and clogged the entrance to its assigned room. In great distress, the thought jumped to the left, to the right, back, forward, drew a short, jagged line containing ellipses, from which hundreds of words rushed to cut in, but it resolutely brushed them aside. It looked for another entrance to its room but found none. It faltered and clasped its hands in despair, grabbed the cluttered word residues and hurled them far away, began to float like a feather and grew and grew, and with it the room.

The Soup

The cooking time for finely chopped blades of grass is three hours; also, move the pot on the stove into direct sunlight, and, if necessary, install a mirror that reflects sunbeams directly into the pot. Be sure to have an emergency generator connected in case of power outages.

Stew the pebbles from the riverbed for twenty-five minutes and then mix them into the soup, add about two pounds of unpeeled garlic, five tablespoons of olive oil and four ounces of freshly fallen snow. During cooking, private conversations are not permitted, as they could distract the approaching afternoon from its further buildup.

Right now, a water bubble is bursting in the pot, some pebbles are hurled out, clap against the tiles behind the stove, stick to them, and slowly slide downwards. At this point, any private conversations are, again, forbidden, as well as utterances of amazement. Next, carefully detach and remove the pebbles from the tiles, place them in the pan with hot oil and lightly fry, vigorously stirring the pot. A few magic spells are indispensable, for instance: "You are a hat in these embers," or, "Comb the mountain and it will turn into a dwarf," or "I am a stone and will act wisely." Repeat three times, and with the third incantation, break into a chant and toss the pebbles, now fried, into the soup.

Suddenly a creaking sound is heard from outside. We rush into the garden and see the collapsed suspension frame of the afternoon, who is shaking violently and clinging desperately to the only tree in the garden, and we look at each other, not knowing what to do, take one step forward, one step back, stretching out our hands to the afternoon, wanting to comfort him, help him back on his feet, and hold him, but first our hands and then our entire bodies just get stuck in the air, while the soup simmers inside.

Deathday

Deathday is lost, buried in piles of trash behind the tin cans and old water bottles, hardly able to breathe, exhausted from years of drudgery and phony announcements; he's fighting for his life. How many times has he sat in the back of a car, manipulated the brakes, swam far out to sea, driven climbers higher up the cliff, to places that proved impossible to scale, causing them to lose their grip and fall? When he finally reached them, the other deathdays cried out, "too late."

And so, after years of humiliation, he looked for an old man without family or anyone else to look after him. Deathday washed his clothes, ironed them, went shopping, read to him from books, cut his hair and his toenails, washed him, wiped his backside, put lotion on his skin, because it was cracked and brittle.

One morning, when deathday came back from the grocery store, the man was no longer there; heart attack, the neighbor told him, he had been taken to the hospital. Deathday drove as fast as he could to see him, and he promptly found him, but another deathday was already sitting on his bed, grinning snidely, bending over the old man and burying him under his weight. When he got back up, the old man had died, and the other deathday ran out of the hospital and into the old man's house. Tears of rage streamed down his face, he busied himself by sorting milk and meat in the fridge and then quickly climbed into the garden towards the cans and old water bottles—everything seemed pointless to him, and yet, he knew that his own deathday would find him. He smiled.

I carry my shadow

I carry my shadow in my armpit so it doesn't get wet and
freeze. The sun, rain showers and wind alternate incessantly,
cooling down the landscape. Our path leads along a
river without a bend—a straight line between the hills,
shimmering silver when the sun shines, becoming a grey
ribbon when rain and snow showers chase across it and when
the wind roughens its surface. According to my compass
we are in the south; it should be hot with sweat flowing
in streams and my shadow walking beside me or rushing
up ahead or visiting a city we come across—I allow it total
liberties, if it comes back from its excursions and lays itself
in bed with me for the night to warm me. Now it's me who
keeps it warm. I fold it gently as it trembles all over from the
cold and shove it in my right armpit.

It's the first time I am carrying it, since I otherwise lie in
its arms like a child and I am held, carried. I can sleep and
dream best this way, counting off my lives and building
heaven, gliding across the glowing sun, but also producing
complete blackness and finally its light, illuminating
everything. We've been on the road for a day now, or has
it been more? Icicles hang from trees into the frozen river
where children ice-skate. How the ice sprays when they
make their curves or suddenly halt. I call to them, but they
don't notice me, even if I dare to get between them on the
ice—it's too thin and breaks under my weight. If I reach out
my hand to say hello, the children don't see me, they will let
me drown. But I always reach the shore without my shadow
waking up or without being sprayed by cold water. It still
sleeps in my armpit, deep and tight.

Now I walk more quickly, and the prospect that it will awake
at the end of the path, helps me forget my exhaustion, and
then we'll switch roles, I will again be the child in its arms,
sleeping, dreaming …

Literal Bewilderment

Bewilderment of the literal kind bears no relationship to the harmlessness of the nursery rhyme, which reduces counting to its essentials. Because it's impossible to do the same thing five times in a row. It's already impossible the second time around, not to mention the third, fourth, and fifth time. There is no second time, everything takes shape anew.

The word is not the same either, even if its clustering of letters, once more, adds up to the same number. Once written down, even if repeated two or three times within the same sentence, it's never the same, in spite of first-glance appearances. Once uttered, the word unfurls its multifarious facets, fans out in accordance with intonation, it's breathless, gently whispered, muted, a slap in the face or a flatterer with delicate skin, soft as a peach, then again a grater that grinds down every face, or indifferent beyond measure, hiding behind other words to gather strength, pulling other words to its side to recite a nursery rhyme; to place a line in mouth and ear: I had a pebble in my shoe and let it skip into the blue, I had a pebble in my shoe and let it skip into the blue, I had a pebble in my shoe and let it skip into the blue ... repeating this line will attenuate bewilderment and bathe things in a crisp and clear light.

First Body Swap

After finalizing the wording of the question that escaped
from the storage shed and just disappeared into the high
grass of the embankment, we're exhausted, lean against
the only tree in the garden, plucking blades of grass,
chewing them, spitting them out, mouths full of saliva and
unspeakable words, but, already, a hand comes to our aid,
and, seemingly inadvertently, touches our hair, her upper
body slightly bends forward, touches a shoulder, a waft of
warm breath fills my nose, my tongue tastes the sweat on her
skin and then the head already does what it must, presses
one cheek against a shoulder, laying all its weight onto it,
and waits, waits for a burst of laughter, for a hand stroking
hair on the head, teasing and yet demanding, and it smells so
sweet, so sweet, the body trembles, no longer knows how to
move, touch where—how—what, eyes closed, and there's the
woman's laughter, closing her hands around his head, holding
it, pulling it towards her, into the smell of wet grass and
sweat and warm breath, towards wide eyes, where tiny veins
meander around in the iris, and she says: kiss me, and lips
begin to press against each other, tips of tongues move into
oral cavities, feeling, entwining, while...

Jackknife dive

When the wound opens, a little blood comes out, and I
quickly soak it up with a sponge, says Night, looking through
the windows of the house. The table in my study is littered
with sharpened pencils and white paper, dried specks of oil
paint everywhere, a brush spreads its stiffened bristles, and
a book left on the small reading table snaps shut and places
itself on the shelf. A door is flung open and falls back into
the lock; still, for a moment I could see the butcher knife
stuck in a loaf of bread on the sideboard, next to freshly
sliced tomatoes and parsley. Quiet piano music is heard
around the house, all the way down to the basement, which
is windowless. This makes the night nervous; she needs to
see everything to be able to obscure it, which requires utmost
concentration. In the garden outside the windowpanes,
she starts to nervously walk up and down, hearing only
the crackling of the snow lying in the garden and covering
everything. Up in the sky, the moon throws herself from
one side to the other and tears her hair; she knows that no
one can help her and finally rolls out of sight. The moon
stopped her visits to earth months ago because her silence
was ignored, everything was garishly lit and shrouded in the
din of slogans, which significantly impaired her sight and
hearing.

Meanwhile, a dung beetle rolls its ball of dung around the
garden, and it keeps getting stuck in the snow, rolls the ball
into a gap in the house facade that widens from the cold, and
it would have loved to tame Night who kept walking back
and forth, and, while they were at it, the table and the pencils
and the white paper and the piano music and the tomatoes
and the parsley, and not to forget the icy windowpanes
covered in snow up to their chins, did their thing.

But everyone was caught unawares when the lantern descended from the park on the hill, and that it would simply push open the gate, cast its dull glow into the garden, make it all the way to the facade and press itself against it. It was a little over the top, the house thought, but of course it still enjoyed the warmth of the lantern ... just then the night threw a fit of rage and pompously pressed a sponge to her forehead, because she had cracked her head against the only tree in the garden, and jumped the garden fence with a jackknife dive into the early dawn.

We Race Across the Viaducts

We race across the viaducts into the tawny colors of autumn. That's all we can make out. We meet up and get in line, and that's all. Our steps now become a river. When we breathe out, the air begins to tremble, it wraps itself around our necks, laces our chests tighter, throws itself into our path and, at the same time, lays out pillows, just in case someone falls. Of course, we race on, we're out of time, and reach new viaducts, which are built from the bones of our ancestors. Our trampling and panting and laughing and screaming wakes them from their sleep. They maintain that they want to have their peace, that they are entitled to it, after all, they have worked hard all their lives; we should have asked them or sent a registered letter announcing our visit, they say, eyeing our skin and flesh.

But we pretend not to notice, in the end we have a right to see our forebears, we only mean well for them and thought it would make for a nice change and show them that they're not forgotten. They have no idea of the trouble we went through to get here: we got lost hundreds of times, crawled through bushes and tickets, swam across rivers, and cascaded down rapids—we never gave up, rescued each other, and now are able to peacefully gaze at the white luminous bones of our ancestors, fragile and yet robust, and contemplate their horny glances—do they know that we've been carrying them in our bodies since birth?

The Last Message

The latest message we just received threatens us with
an irreversible manipulation of our will and a profound
confusion of our sensory impressions. Didn't we just see
an armchair and a table by the side of the road, tightly
embracing each other and tying their legs in a knot? And
right next to them a snail towing an ocean, a huge ship
sailing its waters and high above, a crow picking slices from
the air and rolling them across the sea. And when we enter
the highway rest area, isn't that a polar bear lounging at the
bar, balancing a gumball machine on its snout, with lots
of little creatures that look a lot like us frolicking around
inside it? Has anyone ever seen something like this? And
isn't that a house wall leaping towards our car, but crumbling
immediately at the sight of us? And when we get out of the
car to stretch our legs a bit, isn't that a rooster prancing across
the street, laughing like crazy and turning into stone in front
of our eyes, only to bound away with long leaps and vanish
into the next street. The worst part is the elephant that rides
by on a stag beetle and recites a poem at such a loud pitch
that we must cover our ears. Every now and then a continent
flies by with people standing on it and waving at us. But we
are too confused to wave back at them.

Minutes Later

Minutes later the north was caught in the net cast by the south who was hiding away in a niche in the wall. Coming in from the western gate, the summer strode through the knee-high grass and spread out: clover leaves swirled in the wind, caressing every wall, tree, and shrub, and the fields and the birds on the rooftops. The windows below watched it all with wide-open eyes. And because the summer was generous, he let humans share in it all as well, tenderly stroking their faces, necks, and shoulders.

The summer raised its temperatures slightly, left a few clouds in the sky and got his hair into order. Before moving on, he made the flowers bloom, spread dabs of color across the fields, gave the wind a reddish tinge, as if it was laden with sand.

In passing, the summer glanced at the niche in the wall, where the north now lay peacefully sprawled next to the south and the two were waited on by the west and the east.

Isn't it Strange?

Isn't it strange to imagine the darkness and soap it with light, without it getting any brighter? To dig deeper into the ground and stretch finely braided winds over the hole and mark them with light buoys? And on top of that, to place a few words, as supple night growth, on your eyelashes. To watch them flutter and give shade to the darkness.

Now a new thought comes to rest on your forehead, your skin relaxes. And look, there's a second thought settling down next the first, and another and another. They nestle together, so limber, so soft. I'm perched in the hole, above me the darkness, the whispers of night growth on my eyelids, which are floating skyward with their stories. This longing, this longing for light!

From hearsay

From hearsay we reach into the freezer and pull out a fire extinguisher. The table is set, four chairs, but other than that any further nuisance can be ruled out. Out in the garden the trees are multiplying, and they've decided to pull down the low-hanging clouds. A tadpole from our biotope shares its story before it dives into the deep to live its metamorphosis. A couple of yesterday's impressions haphazardly edge their way forward between the intricately folded napkins on the table and come to rest on the dessert plates. There's a limit to everything. We place the fire extinguisher on the table, a knife and fork at the ready, crossing them. A new sound is born from this collision, one that knows no intervals. We drop the cutlery, everything oscillates around the room—the fire extinguisher and the freezer and the table and the chairs we're sitting on, the carpet, the pictures on the wall, the windowpanes, the kitchen sideboard, the walls...

Every now and then our gaze falls out of the window. Wispy clouds have become entangled in the treetops, someone grabs the fire extinguisher from the table and shoves it into the freezer. We produce a sound with our cutlery, then another. And another, each one different. That way, everything is back in order.

The Heart

The heart takes off his jacket—it's hot—he ties its sleeves to a rib in front of a window in the chest, the one from which he always used to look outside—it's so hot—the window fogs up, the heart can vaguely make out the moon, who looks so sad, and then slides behind a cloud—it's so hot—the heart now takes off his pants, unties the sturdy shoes he always stomps up and down, keeping time with the pistons—it's so hot—sweat bursts from every pore and washes the heart from his place, back and forth, he bounces against the ribs, ever faster and faster, everything races around, the scars are ablaze—it's so hot—and silence settles over everything, the rush of the bloodstreams subsides, the hammering of the pistons that used to pound against the chamber walls dies down ... it was so hot, so silent.

A Dinner

To spread forgotten terminology onto a slice of bread,
you'll need a concrete knife and butter dish, along with
real pressure from an index finger. Background music, deep
breathing, and the scent of sprinkled spices may greatly
facilitate this process. An eye rolls by on the table and comes
to a stop on a leaf of lettuce. Then a second, a third, a fourth
rolls around... While someone practices light reflections
outside in the garden and dusk falls, remindful of the next
morning.

But that should be of no concern to us. Back to the slice
of bread that lies heavy on the plate under the weight of
forgotten terms, surrounded by glasses lisping and chinking
with each other and presumably making fun of the inflated
lungs who, for once, have been allowed into the house.
Meanwhile, the kids play in the garden, twirling through
the air and racing the birds. Three chestnuts and three
cider apples have joined them, jumping around the grass in
excitement. They have no need for legs, their extraordinary
springy elasticity is just as good. Sometimes the kids hang
tear sacs on the cider apples, making them look like human
heads.

Water is poured into the glasses, they are emptied and
emptied and emptied, the slice of bread with its forgotten
terms is broken, passed around, eaten, then burped, and
finally the forgotten terms together with the bread are
digested, and the light is turned off. In bed we remember the
kids sitting in the trees and having a lively discussion with
the night.

A Clean Sweep

Going for a clean sweep, she picks up a pebble from the shore and presses it against her stomach, running the tip of the pebble up and down, scratching deeper into her skin until it bleeds. With her other hand she feels for the spot, runs her fingertips around the landscape of her midsection, descends into regions where no harm can ever come to her, where fear can be released and she can breathe freely. She follows the breath that flows into her body all the way to the tips of her toes and fingers, her lungs open up, inebriated on the air that fills and escapes them. Her body becomes light, floats, and her fingertips keep on tracing the landscape of her torso, leaving it in search for other regions of her skin. There is no longer any need to draw borderlines with pebbles, or to create chasms and artificial rivers. She drops the pebble and gently moves her fingertips across her skin, feeling something softly compelling in her touch, a flow, and then she knows she wants to go on living, that it all becomes a storyline, her storyline, tenderly and clearly.

It's High Time

At one point it takes the shape of a cube that lies
comfortably in the hand, then it's soap bubbles that merge,
growing larger without popping, or it's a word that covers
my face, my chest, that caresses my legs and warms my entire
body, or it's an image of some event, a gesture in the streets,
in the subway, in a room, slips into the heart and keeps still
for a few moments, takes on clear outlines and is carried by
the blood stream into every corner of the body, vibrating
along nerve tracts—and all of this exists only for fractions of
a never ending second—and this picture fills the spaces of
the body, the world, for this moment that will never end!

Every Rhythm

Every rhythm tells a different story. Be it dipped in mutton
fat, prepared with strong meat broth, sautéed in a skillet,
wrapped in bay leaves, drenched in olive oil, stuffed into a
beef roulade—when consumed, the rhythm penetrates any
worn out brain, stretches limbs and makes them light, or
heavy, shortens and expands intervals, refines with garlic,
adds sugar, a little sage, then curry, is chaos with a down-to
earth tongue. Rhythm spreads out, becomes a body inside
the body, produces secretions, settles on languishing palates
in need of replenishment, plops down into the tormented
stomach with its falling rocks and pockets of embers, attends
public executions in the intestines, takes it all in, shy, primed
for violence, voracious, gentle, and unsentimental...

He Who Calls Himself God

Why does he call himself God? He can't even tuck a flower behind his ear. The trees are strange to him, he is terribly afraid of house windows—eyes evil, he slurs, eyes evil. When we get to a bend in the road, he drops to his knees, sticks his index fingers in his ears and lowers his head, moving his lips, closing his eyes as if praying devoutly, and refuses to move from his spot. He doesn't give a damn if we have to bring in heavy salvage equipment and slave away for days to haul him away. Not to mention the costs and energy use this involves.

But the next day he's back, shunning the streets and crashing every party, no matter how well it's hidden away. Of course, he can hardly keep himself upright, staggers like a drunkard, and stares holes into the air. When asked to leave, he cracks an obtuse smile. And so, the party relocates to another venue, in hopes of not being bothered there.

He shows no reaction to people that happen to pass by, most likely because he only perceives them as blotches of color moving through the landscape. He's not keen on personal hygiene. At night when the moon shines bright, he is shaken by crying fits, which are broadcast via invisible loudspeakers into the landscape where we must work and live. At that point, sleep is out of the question, it's impossible to have normal conversations, because the crying fits of the one who calls himself God drowns out all other sounds. In these nights we huddle in our houses, eyes turned to the sky, counting the stars, stroking our hair for encouragement, and waiting for the morning to come. With the first light of dawn, the crying fits fade away, we rise, relax, and loosen our bodies and walk out into the day, past the deep hollow that has filled with water, where he who calls himself, God knelt all night, crying a tiny sea where today our kids sail their little paper boats.

The Day of Your Birth

When somebody pushes your bed out of the house and all you see is his shadow above you, with rain passing through it and pelting your face, perhaps a treetop flitting by high above you, the glowing threads of your past life in its branches— then let things take their course. The wreath that is pushed onto your little head smells like wet wool dried on a stove. There's no need to feel embarrassed when you are washed and dressed, and your bed rolls out into the fields.

Slide forward an infinite distance as the bed sinks into the damp earth. No more shadow bent over you. No sky. No star as you sink deeper, and earth begins to cover your eyes. You'll stay there until tomorrow, deep down in the soil, enjoy it, because you'll no longer be able to lie so still later on. Can you hear the hurried footsteps, the screaming, the laughter, can you feel the tears on your face? — that will be the day of your birth.

Take The Feather from The Ox

Take the feather from the ox to stroke the crescent moon in your lap. Try not to tickle it as things are imaginably bad: rocks break off from the mountains and fill up the valleys, trees die off and the rivers drown in the seas. Do you hear that subtle grinding? It's the sand grating the air until it's sore. Then there's the taunting howl of the winds—the choir should sing of your ending.

The pea underneath your skin is no longer useful. The crow's nest in your lung offers no protection and the abused confession in your spleen is blessed by a dung beetle in search of its shoes. Here! Catch the house flying by as its inhabitants lie awake in their beds and refuse to fill the night with their dreams. They don't care and many hope they will no longer wake up; they've become so numb.

Let the flies out of your breast, let them span threads in the air and climb up them higher and higher and shake up the clouds floating by. Wave to the crescent moon, assure it you will return and that it will always have a place in your lap. Wave to the crying rooster standing all alone on the dung pile, wave until your arm hurts. Then glide down the flies' threads, lay the crescent moon back in your lap, take the shadow from your arm and spread it flat on the floor to throw him over any passers-by, to warm or cool it according to the weather, and from the crescent moon you will pull an umbrella embellished with shells and bright corals. Don't be shocked if this includes dead fish.

And harken preferably to the trousers laughing, flapping like flags on the legs of the passers-by. And don't be disappointed about the pair of trousers wrapping itself around the crescent moon and taking it along. Rejoice in the river, flowing quietly by, sometimes mumbling a word, a syllable, that laps onto the shore. Then the time has come for you to think over carefully whether you rub your winter boots at home with garlic, wrap them in parchment paper and carry them into the cellar, or what is more important—whether you want to nurture the frying pan in the kitchen, where—like a cracked open egg— the new year is already sizzling.

The Body at the River

He lies on his back—the back of his head in the river. He
doesn't answer questions, speaks only with his naked body
stuck in papery skin. Delicate tears extend and branch out
over his skin on the underarms and legs. Taking a more
careful look, you recognize regular signs, like letters, most of
them practically faded; allusions, which seem to balance on
the tears and remind of a text, covering the body entirely, its
history, undecipherable to us. A spiral on the belly is etched
deeply into the skin, a solar plexus, the navel lies in its middle
in a small hole. The throat and facial skin only display vertical
lines, which lead around the eye sockets to unite into a point
on the forehead.

His shoes and socks and shirt and trousers lie back in the
bushes, including the picnic basket with the song book
full of children's songs among broken plates and glasses.
Forest berries get moldy at the bottom of the basket. With
eyes wide open, the body observes the sky, scattered clouds
chasing across it. Birds draw lines, ellipses, and amplitudes in
the air, which cool off in the evening.

He's been lying these ways for days without changing
position. Sometimes we have the impression he is listening,
waiting for a certain tone or sound, which allows him to get
up and walk. On our daily walks we take our rest with him,
observe him, eat, and drink, study the texture of his skin,
and let ourselves fall in the stillness exuding from him. We
sit that way for hours, but at the end we are disappointed
that his breast doesn't rise and fall. Though he is alive in our
dreams, he runs, jumps, walks, speaks with a voice we carry
around with us all day long. Something else we do, he is with
us—we sense that, and it feels strange. We still shy away
from his cold leathery skin.

Today we tickle the soles of his feet, which are filthy. We wash his feet with water from the river and lay them to dry in the sun. The texture in the soles of the feet emerges as if it had just been etched into the skin, and then we realize that those are marks from our washing, our scratches from removing a persistent stain, the pressure points from our fingers from grasping the feet as we washed.

From the legs a bit of blood comes, forms drops, which dry quickly in the sun, and the tulip, growing from his belly blooms in white, moves, sways to the side, left, right, as if a strong wind were blowing. All is peaceful here—only the flowing of the river. The carnation reminds of a blossomed phallus, and one of us, the strongest, tries to pull it out, we help him take hold of the pelvis and pull on it. But although we make quite an effort, the tulip remains tightly implanted in the belly. When we hand each other tissues for wiping off our sweat, the body lets out a sigh, gargling, rattling; we don't know what to do, for a moment we believe our treatment has driven him to this, we already want to congratulate ourselves that we have conjured up this reaction in him, and—the dried drops of blood sparkle briefly in the sun, become dull, and fade in the skin.

The body pays no attention to us. We hold a compact mirror in front of his mouth, nothing happens, someone tickles the soles of his feet, no reaction. Suddenly one of us grabs the feet, twists them, lifts them up and lets them fall on the ground. He wants to kick them, looks for a stick on the riverbank to beat them. We hold him back, go with him to the edge of the forest, set him on moss—he cries, his body trembles, we wrap our arms around him, stroke his hair but he will not be soothed.

In the meantime, some others dedicate themselves to the body at the river. They try to cross his arms across his chest by applying all their strength in lifting them up, bending them, and placing them on the breast. Whenever they let go of the arms, the arms rush back to their previous position. They try this three or four times, then they leave them alone and walk to the crying one at the edge of the forest, who is lying on his back with overflowing eyes. With eyes overflowing.

At the bank we illuminate the body's eyes with a flashlight. They don't blink but stay wide open. Thousands of little blood vessels in them have burst, covering both eyes in a murky fluid, and sealing them, as it were. We are convinced the body has fallen asleep and is dreaming its endless dream, revisiting his distant past. Children float across the river on a raft they made themselves. They wave, call, laugh—we wave back and get ready to leave, clearing away our garbage. Will the body still be here tomorrow?

from *The night is silent backwards*

Booby traps and other ribaldries

We've been floating in murky waters since yesterday—with a rigid backbone and stiff knees. The booby traps in our heads are nowhere to be found. Furthermore, last night's corridors are closed and hold the light captive. We pull out the periscope, wipe the oculars clean and pluck unruly hairs from eyebrows. In the meantime, a grating voice announces from the ship's loudspeaker that the fruit on the trees on land is ripening, the fields are completely harvested, and fish are washed onto the beach on certain sections of the coast; we should also finally trip the booby traps in our heads before going on land to collect new impressions. We, naturally, ignore this request and listen to the voice that speaks of the sea glittering in the sunlight, the measuring unit 23, which accelerates our thought processes. As always, the same text, and finally the voice from the loudspeaker burns things from long ago into our heads, while it gushes on in indulgent depictions of light spectrums, rambling about the shadow of things, which bring about rooms underneath the top of the skull, and that we should finally use these, simply for a change of pace. This is annoying, and we only wait for the silencing of the voice, which loosens the nerves in our brains, and we finally find the booby traps in our heads and defuse them, before we go on land.

Breach of contract

For the time being, the horizon may not be minimized, although it is rapidly advancing. The paint on the strutting has not dried, the glowing lights not delivered, because the coordinates speed through the air and won't calm down, but what weighs down on us most heavily is that the night, which should take away all perspective, does not come for another two weeks: this is a clear breach of contract. Only the night could have calmed the horizon. This is depressing and demands consequences. All available construction machinery is summoned to contain the horizon's assault through the excavation of deep ditches. The mere beginning of operations is sobering: the sun is ablaze in the sky and impedes every movement, the horizon quakes, strikes continuously faster waves for its next assault. We fear for our health, the first breakdowns set in, first indentations and bulges on our bodies are detected, identified by touch. To not see, our eyes seek refuge behind dense veils. What use are the words, assurances, blames gushing out of everyone while straying among the construction machinery. They are exactly as forlorn as we are, while the air shimmers restlessly and the scorching sun presses everything into the sand—only the horizon remains. This state lasts infinitely long, but suddenly the wind springs up, runs against the horizon, breaks its strutting, and carries it away.

Making inhabitable

Only when the pending geometry assignments are resolved, by setting circles and isosceles triangles free, only then will we comprehend that this accumulation of lines, circles, angles, including their medieval strongholds, wield great influence on our thinking and behaviour. One still crucifies, rectifies, roughens, brandishes, sharpens, although the delineated vanished long ago is no longer tangible, only lives on in our memory as pale spectres, generating the feeling of a cold-blooded prison, where we must perfect the calculations and line management of our lives. Since the transitions constantly evade, we indulge in routine contradictions: addresses and arrivals are exchanged and swapped with extraordinary grace, cloudy confusions for the fencing bout are cheered up with their reflections, moist spots licked up with the tongue to perchance make our adult streams of consciousness still inhabitable.

Establishing

Let's establish the distances again and merge the fireplaces.
Let's scatter ourselves. Let's find ourselves. We shun
the walls' clumsy approaches and mistrust the doorsteps'
promises, anchored in every nook and cranny. The dead do
not answer for us; that's right, they never have, and who
knows whether they are indeed dead. That's right. That's
why we can no longer cry and are sure that everything we
now see and experience is from long ago, or will take place
anytime soon. This makes us irresolute, that's why our arms
hang down to the ground, our hands stir up earth, we bend
our backs and shut our eyes. Leaves rustle, shrubs next to the
narrow path bow over us and graze our hair, as if they wanted
to console us. If we turn around, we recognize faces in the
leafage; arms, hands, and legs briefly jump out of the bush
and then jump back in again. And we trip along the path like
this, and don't want to get lost. We see the horizon kneeling,
praying for permission to leave.

Welcome change of pace

We follow well, apparently, the cold spurs us on, we'll be up there right away. Then we'll see what happens. We will not describe the climactic details, there would be no point. We don't know the names of the plants and minerals but are poised for each cardinal direction. As it is we are content when it's no longer steep, since we have the feeling that something is shifting in us, something about the near future and it is of greatest significance. Of course, we can't see it. The path now goes imperceptibly downhill, toward our starting point. Even the fact that it's beginning to snow is no coincidence. We must raise our feet higher to proceed, stopping often out of breath, snow reaching up to our knees. Somewhere it's ringing. We go south. It should be warm there. The path continues to be long, it takes its time with us, shoving snow to its edges and casting us off right into the snow several meters deep, this wet grave, where we do not freeze, and can no longer pursue each onward path.

Swift contemplation

Contemplate swiftly, then switch directions in slow steps, past the shadows lying on the snow. Trees break away from the nearby forest, glide through the snow several meters deep to the crest of the hill. Sounds from all around meet each other in silence. Whoever comes too late may only keep the right angle of their own nakedness and thighs with deep creases—incredible how much resistance this contains. Despite the faltering handstands in the wind, reaching the wooden house goes smoothly to then open the door and to hope for the nourishment of a bed, a blanket, where hands which envelop and are warm wait underneath. There are no games to lose here, even when water invades followed by detritus, while snow still lies several meters deep outside. The blanket rustles in the sudden cold, aroused hands skip on fingertips over sheets. Flowers in the vases on the windowsill chime their bells, and round handwriting gathers on the opposite wall, adorning itself with the remaining blood from last spring, spreading it on the skipping hands before the detritus shimmies over it.

The soul's gravity

The soul's gravity has abandoned its function. Torches with clouds of smoke are quickly thrust into the earth; they don't warm or spread light, rather their smoke should hinder the upcoming surveying for the tomb. An additional measure is not available. A ring of keys jingles somewhere. Shoe heels tap on asphalt in front of the house. The bodies present in the front room announce future absences and leave the rooms with black backpacks stuffed with outmoded views and convictions, which they bury in the garden in front of the house, while branches from the nearby oak tree scratch the windowpanes like crazy. The wind is extraordinary, heavy raindrops burst on the asphalt; clouds hang low. Necks do not want to stay here to be kissed, caressed, or to begin any form of entertainment. Instead, painted wooden signs are put up to point out the discontinuation of all action. As if to confirm in a last act of revolt, the wind tosses little underpants from the laundry line onto the wet grass. Silhouettes appear on the garden fence. Smoky torches in hands are thrust onto the grave of outmoded views and convictions. The silhouettes straighten themselves and devoutly grasp the hands, observed by their last hour, which stands helplessly at the attic window. This here and now does not fit in its memory; it trembles from its own tension and lets all periods for an objection elapse while the silhouettes climb to it up the wooden staircase.

A protocol

We continue the protocol on each of our steps so the terrific speed of the change in location does not overwhelm us, and we carelessly overlook something. And, as we reach the attic to dedicate ourselves to the last hour, a new image presents itself yet again. An image of us walking through a forest, someone wants to say something, we see nothing, we don't understand anything, we stop briefly to hear better. When we leave the forest, a sandy beach suddenly lies ahead of us; above it is a scorching sun, and we've hardly put up the first umbrellas, we side-slip in the sand, tumble down an incline, we splash into a river, sinking deeper, are set adrift, floating in cold water, and some think we overlooked an important moment earlier, and cannot possibly be there where we would need to be, we really should be up in the attic ... but we sit with dripping wet hair at coarsely constructed wooden tables in a restaurant garden, pencils in our right hands, erasers in our left hands, graph paper on the table in front of us. We know we cannot write anything meaningful under these burdensome conditions, but we do it anyway. To distract ourselves we call a waiter, but no one comes. So, we continue writing. The meaning of each written word remains incomprehensible, but we continue, convinced that through this an order arises which holds us firm. This way we can welcome each new connection the words form, likewise all changes in direction, each newly arising play of colors with the morphing of the landscape; and the wonderful thing, we lose ourselves in the sounds and rhythm of the words, we begin to run—highly erected, crouched, sashaying. But the words remain uncatchable, refusing any conversation, or touching as well; the consequence is that many of us lay their

heads on the fully written sheets of paper and fall asleep,
pencils and erasers fall from our hands; when their wet hair
has dried, many wake up, speak of gorgeous encounters
with words, of heartfelt touches, the vibrations of these are
still tangible, of a constant new forming, intertwining, and
exuding, a constant coming and going, in secret, perceptibly;
and everywhere rooms expand, contract ... and there will be
no end.

Conversation with Stones

This rain is not to be underestimated. It simply wipes many sounds from the air, patters on raincoats and umbrellas while we sink with each step into the moist earth up to our ankles. Tracks follow us, rush ahead, betray us. So, we change direction. We don't want well-trodden paths and to constantly subject ourselves to the tracks' deliberate confusion. The climate here is not beneficial for our undertaking although it rains ceaselessly. Of course, we've insisted on this desert expedition, which we've been planning meticulously for years. It's not our fault that the landscape we've come upon appears different from the desert depicted in the photographs. This allows us to walk more freely, even when we sink up to our knees with each step. Each time we stop due to exhaustion, a dune sails by, covered by the small craters the rain has beaten in the sand—it's like the dune in the textbook we studied for this expedition; it's the same for the stones, which lie about in the thousands and have been washed clean by the rain; they accompany us. When we sit down on them, we begin to immediately converse with them as if we were old acquaintances. We avoid anything arbitrary, the same for meaningless questions and answers, or self-indulgent monologues. We sit on the stones for hours, feel their even breath, which transposes our bodies into vibration; we simply listen, understand, speaking is not necessary, we hearken, stand up and walk slowly onward. The stones follow us, glide through the sand, plow the desert.

They really exist

Assuming they really exist: these fans of light in the air with their steel radiance trembling like water in a glass on the table. Assuming. Did we expect something different, does the room have to be deserted all at once? Or if a lantern with a soft light moves through the night, takes each of its steps deliberately, stops time after time to listen carefully and to sense the cool breeze from the brook flowing by with its slender body —would that in the end be considered an unauthorized removal from the workplace? Or if a random 200 kilo man on the street places himself on one of the stretched out lower arms of a fallen passer-by, if he neither sees nor senses this, and slowly wipes his ears and nose with rumpled tissue while teetering restlessly back and forth, because the cleaning process isn't going smoothly, resulting in the lower arm below the shoes of the 200 kilo man being veritably crushed, would one be obligated to intervene or can one simply continue walking and attempt to erase this image from one's memory? Or when just after vomiting the nausea comes, nesting itself for hours in the belly, and is only soothed by tapping signals on the forehead; and still comes and goes, as it sees fit, and hooks itself in the oesophagus … should one be worried about one's health? Or if someone wants to forcibly stretch out a too minimal distance with the aid of steel clamps and ropes, should one drive them away with glaring headlights and loud music before they can even begin this madness? These questions relieve our stay in this world. Sometimes this brightens the murkiness up and our hearts beat more peacefully.

And this, too

We were cut open three times, stitched up, brought from the city, and placed in a wheat field; then the vocal cords were stretched, white sheets spread over us, weighed down with stones. Days later, hunger lured us out from under the sheets. We crept across the wheat field, saw a village, got ourselves on our feet, and walked among the farmyards without meeting a human. In the barns we found buckets full of water that we guzzled away from the screaming cattle—one needs to live from something. Now we think of our arrival, while we stuff our mouths full of loamy soil and sawdust. This naturally has an impact on the digestion including the subsequent discharge. Not a pretty sight. During the day we walk back and forth in the farmyards with stomach cramps, we are silent, closing window shutters that were left open, which we open again at night—though we never cast a glance in the rooms, which emit the regular breathing from sleeping people. This breathing accompanies us through the darkness and brings us into a contemplative state, keeping us up until the crack of dawn. We've become thirsty and run into the stalls and again slosh up the water in the tin buckets meant for the cows. Finally, we cheer on the cows to shove the straw away with their hooves. When we lay ourselves in the hollow they've created, their udders dangle over us and the stomach cramps stop.

Passwords

If the answer is a yes, we will glide into loving arms, it's this
way even among wolves and foxes, and then the claim comes
naturally, at some point to be washed from the embraces into
overcrowded stairwells. It's that simple. Many swimmers
do not realize that water causes wetness. They sit amazed in
puddles, increasing the collection of dust on the stairs, which
leads to deepening to things through the general restlessness
of the crack. The stairwell is crowded with hands, elbows,
and knees, which push, feet that kick. Many dip the tips of
their fingers into the murky water and then lick them. We
rise every hour and pull ourselves on the railing one floor up.
This goes on all day, constantly whirred about by hands, arms,
legs. Once we finally reach the top, we avoid intimate looks,
since this could be misunderstood. Only when dawn shines
it light dirty on the horizon, do we dare to sit on the railings,
and observe the appendages, lying below us exhausted on
the floor. What should we think of this? Life strains, and
it would be unbearable if we didn't have passwords hidden
in our tufts of hair, which we pull out and hurtle into the
morning light until the air brightens up.

No property

No property, just knots lying on top of each other, which extend more tightly every day. No one knows who they belong to. That must be acknowledged if we want to continue; otherwise we'll become cruel, surround ourselves as our own enemies, spend our lives in the concocting of plans for slaughter, which, once implemented, spin out of control. In exceptional cases, death is desirable, but not necessary. The guzzling of food becomes a holy duty, not one body is spared from this, increasing the discombobulated operations. Then it can happen, that the core is yanked out, hammered through, reduced to small pieces, and then torn with greedy teeth, or someone is pressed by a thumb on the forehead for so long until a deep dent is formed. This is unbearable to look at, we sink our gazes, barricade them with hands and plastic tapes, walk over here and over there, but constantly return, until by chance a way out appears: since we see nothing more, we slide over a slope, directly into a lake, which graciously receives us and we spend the coming days under water, and this calms us—hovering there in one singular embrace.

Expectation

As long as the dim sun goes astray among the clouds,
all is not yet lost. The official hours are extended.
Misunderstandings support themselves on the balustrade of
wooden balconies and observe the queues, which peter out
in the horizon. No one is appreciative of that. The opening
on the city square is embellished with brightly colored
flowerpots, canvases painted with densely standing trees are
hoisted. Everything here should appear natural. The step
sequences of shy deer are measured and constantly adjusted
to the guidelines until new contexts arise; conversations
are either held off record or brandished back and forth on
giant posters. A bedpost still shines up from the underbrush;
woollen sweaters lie on the streets without anger, a pair
of shoes slides along, following the February afternoon,
which is just now crossing over the city square, scattering
snowflakes—that can be a good beginning. No wonder that
everyone who can walk, creep or crawl, collects at the city
square to erect the gigantic tent, where they wait for spring.

Preparing salmon

Noon is appeased, flies slain, grass cut, the cows in front
of the window are filled with Johann Sebastian Bach—all
done with lively sensitivity, as it should be for our situation.
This constellation could degenerate into further flowery
arrangements, increasing our admiration for the salmon
on the cutting board. This makes everything velvety and
encourages the slicing process to begin: there should
be little morsels with a pinch of salt and olive oil. This
naturally includes counter movements: blatant vanities
which scrupulously wrangle space and call for the use of
cheap vinegar and crude herbs. To avoid this, we situate
the centre of our wanting on the tips of knives next to the
cutting board, open all the doors in the house and wait for
whomever wants to support us. Gender and appearance are
unimportant, likewise age. Since we are open for any aid.
The main thing is that this filet of salmon lying in front of
us remains. We stand unswervingly in front of the cutting
board, drafting with our eyes the first slicing attempts across
the salmon, which the tip of the knife will shortly follow,
without mercy, and we would be lying if in doing so we were
joyless.

It's rumbling at the location. Its hiccup chases shadows into
the country and light gusts of wind finally carry them off.
Soon the first exhausted ones will also be hastily buried.
Reasons as far as the eye can see. On a case-by-case basis, the
location will hang on a tree in front of the window as soon as
tomorrow. Its discourses to the snow, the embarrassment of
this, soothe me. I join company with it and take a seat on it.
It doesn't give me any assignment, leaves further steps up to
me, spans the bridges from a to b and has them subsequently

ending nowhere. Hands lie naked in the snow. They shovel snow for hours.

One easily becomes suspect as a fanatic searching for the words' miserable hideouts. This is also an advantage to my position. The suspect remains suspicious und is ultimately nowhere to be found. That's why this location where I've resided for two weeks has grown dear to me.

If I should I graze a wall, then I'll also graze the second, the third, the fourth. Light falls through the cracks. Warm light swirling with particles of dust. Before bedtime the fields freeze into sleep, face and ears floating on the echoes of night. Life and death are for nothing here. The bright areas have become frequent.

In The Machinery Room

We have covered our exterior with white stone tiles, the
staircases have no doors, the double windows are shut
tight. Ticking machines in the reception hall, their endless
dialogues are morse code for the wind, blowing the morning
mist about. An access road twists up from the brush in the
forest, smells of damp earth. Hands sketch clouds, smear
them on mirrors and uncover extensive cellar frames. This
triggers momentary discontent, as many feel caught off
guard and sense complex patterns of animosity on their skin.
These remain admittedly invisible, but the threats intensify,
nipping each reconciling gesture in the bud, stretching,
tightening, drilling. Then noone stands on their own legs
anymore: the movements conduct themselves in a circle, until
they are quietly exhausted. Red herrings are displayed on
top of the cellar frames; the ticking of the machines in the
reception hall gets louder. Glistening wine in glass carafes
remains untouched on the only table. Suddenly a gust of
wind forces the closed windows open and blows into the
house yellow sketch books in which patterns of movement
are drawn carefully hatched. This gives great pleasure, and we
immediately chip off the white stone tiles from our bodies to
feel the draft on our skin from the patterns of movement in
the sketch books.

No Mere Hunger

This rippling and surging, above us the domed shade of the chestnut tree woven with silver threads moving the wind in waves—a grey restless sea. Muffled explosions deep below us: blades of grass tremble in stone mortice, the clacking of shoe heels becomes faster; we hear panting very close as if someone were fleeing, and we begin to tense the muscles in our bodies, want to jump up, but it doesn't work, we cannot move. Hunger forces us to silence—though words always find their way over our lips. We constantly wonder how this hunger found entry into our bodies. We are still able to distract ourselves by talking about how it used to be, about the windows without glass in our cottage in the forest, about the cows and dogs that went astray that we cared for and nourished until they were taken away from us again, by the farmers, the police, by the disappearing of the cows and the dogs, because they believed they would have it better somewhere else, and again and again we have to tell our bodies of the wilted bouquets of flowers on our terrace, the ones we were convinced were whispering to us; and sometimes we did not emerge from nodding our heads and laughing; that's how good we felt, indifferent to the fog, snow, rain, warmth, cold: our bodies accepted it, and still today we admire this about them. Now hunger complains again, although it has direct access to our ears, which it blasts with sounds of screaming, slobbering, the smacking of lips, before it burrows itself through our bodies in search of an overseen crumb. It's constantly in motion and distracts us from forming a clear thought. Instead, we must watch as words clump together, bogging down our streams of consciousness while hunger rumbles in our bodies.

Capsizing

There, as clear as day, perhaps the final syllable is the only weakness, while the other syllables amplify the vibrations in our bodies. We don't admit the thought that we may be dealing with two different sets of facts. We shoo this possibility away like a pesky fly and write it off as a natural departure. Likewise, the expansive rooms where nothing objectively, horizontally, vertically exists, where even the restoring of the initial situation and the implementation of new measuring units is of no help. We persevere for a time, proceed with new work, and vehemently resist any inactivity. We enjoy the new illusions, which transcend their design and spend days excavating ditches where we wander around; these lead us into the past and force us into intense conversations with our ancestors. Thereby forms of annotations materialize, leading us to draw false conclusions as we have no actual inkling of the contents of these conversations and the stillness between tones is hard for us to bear. Luckily, stories from our lives hurry to our aide, which distract, blur, and in doing so bring about an undertow, washing us into the glistening light of all phenomena, shining in darkness, illuminating the way out of the ditches.

Differences

The climate's impact on the soul is not to be underestimated.
Mucous membranes suffer especially and even the
deftest pair of lovers experiencing this will avoid entering
unknown rooms. Should this happen by chance, it has
serious ramifications on birth and mortality rates, aside
from the resulting unforeseeable, sharp-angled changes in
directions, which ensue. Many lead to cold rippling water
with exuberant fish populations, others directly to incessant
echoes of shrill voices surging against jagged cliffs. This is
unnerving, and not even quick steps may be of help. Once
the clear mind kicks in again, deaths and births commence
immediately. Shrugging reports about this remain in the
background before they turn toward new bodies and things,
which pass by ecstatically and find themselves again in an
intimate embrace or repulsion.

Publication of Miniatures since...

2013 *IDIOME* nr.6 – sechs Miniaturen.

2014 *Austr(al)ia, Prosa aus Australien und Österreich, Anthologie im Rahmen der 13th*. International Conference on the Short Story – 5 Miniatures in English. Translation: Hillary Keel.

"Unbraiding the Short Story", edited by Maurice Lee, *Anthology – 5 Miniatures in English*. Translation: Hillary Keel.

Die Rampe 4/ 2014 - Miniaturen.

Literatur und Kritik 489, November 2014 – Miniaturen.

2015 *Die Rampe* 4/2015 – neue Miniaturen.

2016 *Der Standard, Album*, 13. 2. 2016 – Gedicht „Zwang".

Firebord 3 – „zu 100 Jahre DADA" – Miniatur „Eine Verwechslung".

Die Rampe 4/2016 – neue Miniaturen.

2017 *Literatur & Kritik* 517, September 2017 – Miniaturen.

Manuskripte 217, September 2017 – Miniaturen.

FLASH The International Short-Story Magazine, 2017 – "I carry my Shadow". Translation: Hillary Keel https://storefront.chester.ac.uk/images/101editorial.pdf

Schlussbilanz/Final balance – Anthologie des Linzer Frühling – Miniaturen. https://www.bibliothekderprovinz.at/media/leseprobe/schlussbilanz_30_jahre_linzer_fruehling_lsp.pdf

2021 *WordCity Literary Magazine*, Canada. https://wordcitylit.ca/2021/12/15/wordcity-literary-journal-april-2021-issue-8/

www.ingramcontent.com/pod-product-compliance
Lightning Source LLC
Chambersburg PA
CBHW030344030726
47499CB00003B/889